The PIRATE ANGEL,
The TALKING TREE,
and Captain
RABBIT

STEVE BEHLING

Los Angeles · New York

First Edition, April 2019

10 9 8 7 6 5 4 3 2 1

FAC-020093-19046

Printed in the United States of America

Designed by Kurt Hartman

Cover illustration by Veronica Fish

Library of Congress Control Number: 2018962994

ISBN: 978-1-368-04695-4

Visit www.DisneyBooks.com

and www.Marvel.com

CHAPTER 1

"Hey, don't touch that!"

The voice belonged to Rocket. As did everything else aboard the ship.

Rocket could put up with just about anyone or anything, as long as anyone or anything stayed out of his way.

But one look at Thor Odinson, and it was pretty clear to him that that guy was most definitely *in* the way.

When Rocket saw Thor Odinson move a hand toward the vessel's master control panel, he drew the line. He didn't care if the guy was a man, or a god, or the beautiful child of a pirate and an angel.

"I wasn't going to touch anything," said

Thor, his tone suggesting that he most certainly was considering *exactly* that.

Rocket arched his right eyebrow, his lip curled into a sneer. "You can't lie to a liar," Rocket said. "Just don't get near any of the controls. They're all very delicate, like your facial features." He bared his teeth in an approximation of a grin.

"I do not have delicate facial features," Thor protested, slightly defensive.

"C'mon, they are," Rocket jabbed. "A little delicate. It's okay, there's nothing wrong with that."

"I am Groot."

Rocket whipped his head around, nearly colliding with the adolescent treelike alien standing right behind him. Groot had a knack for sneaking up on people, just one of the annoying habits he'd acquired since whatever this pubescent phase could be called had overtaken the young tree with a vengeance.

"Hey, what did I tell you about insulting our guest?" Rocket scolded, shaking his head.

"If anyone's gonna do any insulting around here, it's gonna be me."

Groot looked at Rocket, and enacted an impressive—albeit obnoxious—imitation of the same sneer that Rocket used on Thor just a few seconds earlier.

"I am—"

"Don't finish that sentence," Rocket warned.

"Gr—"

"I mean it! You wanna have tablet privileges revoked for a week, you go right ahead and finish that thought."

If Groot had pockets, he would have shoved his limbs stubbornly into them, turned around grumbling, and walked away. As it was, he didn't, so after a moment's stare-off with Rocket he simply muttered, "I am Groot," then ambled away.

"He's in an awkward phase," Rocket said to Thor by way of explanation, turning his attention to the master control panel.

"Adolescence is never easy," Thor said, looking over Rocket's shoulder. "I remember when Loki and I were children. Loki transformed himself into a snake, and because I really, really loved snakes, I went to pick it up. But the moment I did, the snake transformed back into Loki, and then he stabbed me."

It was at least ten seconds before Rocket spoke. And when he finally did, he sighed and said, "Why do I have the feeling you tell this story a lot? Like, A LOT."

Thor smiled wanly. "Maybe a few times," he acknowledged.

"I bet this Loki gets a big kick out of it every time you tell it," Rocket said, chuckling.

The thin smile on Thor's face quickly fell.

"Not anymore" were the only words Thor could manage before he turned away.

Rocket and Thor had known each other for only a few hours. They had met under poor circumstances, which were the only circumstances that Rocket seemed to know these days.

The Guardians of the Galaxy had picked up a distress call from an unknown vessel, and traveled to its last-known coordinates on a desperate rescue mission. Well, maybe the motivation for the mission wasn't quite so much rescue as it was the potential of receiving a huge reward. The ship's coffers were running low, and expeditious as always, the crew was looking to do good—but also to store up some funds.

But when they arrived, the Guardians found nothing but debris floating through space. And corpses. It seemed like anyone who had been aboard the distressed craft had been killed by person or persons unknown.

Or at least that's what they'd thought, until someone had slammed into the Guardians' cockpit.

Bringing the survivor aboard, Rocket and the Guardians had learned that the man/god/child of a pirate and an angel's name was Thor, and he was an Asgardian. They'd also learned that the ship in distress was Asgardian in origin, and it had been destroyed by Thanos.

Thanos, the so-called Mad Titan.

Rocket thought Thanos was a real jerk. Not just for destroying the Asgardian ship and all its occupants, though there was that. No, Rocket thought he was a jerk for everything he had done to Rocket's fellow Guardian and friend, Gamora, daughter of Thanos.

He had heard firsthand what Gamora had gone through under Thanos's watch, beginning from the time Thanos had killed half of her people, the Zehoberei, and taken Gamora as his adopted "daughter." He pitted Gamora against another "daughter," Nebula, engaging them in a deadly rivalry designed to turn both of them into perfect killing machines.

It worked. And for a long time, it had cost the two women their souls.

Jerk.

"You're in a foul mood, rabbit," Thor said, shaking his head.

"I'm in a foul mood? Yeah, I wonder why," Rocket said sarcastically. Surely it had nothing to do with pirate-angel progeny constantly mistaking him for a rabbit.

"I am Groot," said the tree, trying to steal a look over Rocket's shoulder.

The diminutive Guardian quickly clutched the tablet to his chest, and got up from his seat. "Stop sneaking up on people like that!" Rocket yelled. "How many times do I gotta tell you? It's creepy!"

"I am Groot."

"Ugh. Ever since you got a little sap, you're a total brat," Rocket said as he walked over to a bin, and deposited the tablet safely within.

"Why do I have the feeling that you say that to him a lot," Thor interjected. "Like, *a lot.*"

Rocket stared daggers at Thor. "Are you makin' fun of me?"

"No," Thor said innocently. "Of course not."

"Yes, you are," Rocket replied. "You're mocking me."

"Not at all," Thor added.

"Yeah, right!" Rocket snapped. "You're mimicking me!"

"I am Groot," piped up Groot from his swivel chair.

"Stay out of this, tree," Thor said.

Rocket poked a finger right in Thor's face. "Hey! You can't talk to him like that! Only I can talk to him like that." He turned to Groot. "Stay outta this, tree!"

"I am Groot."

Rocket sat back down, slumped in his seat, and closed his eyes. "Hah. Wait'll I tell Gamora about you and that mouth of yours."

CHAPTER 2

Rocket was busy.

He was preoccupied tinkering with the pod, and Groot realized it was a great opportunity to snatch the tablet Rocket had been using and see what kind of games he had on it. Maybe there was something really good, something that would help pass the time on this super-boring flight to wherever it was they were going.

Groot chanced a glance over at the Thor guy, but he was busy staring out of the cockpit into space, his face looking as though his mind was a million miles away. Groot thought about maybe saying something to him.

Nah. It was finally time for Groot to have some fun. For all of Rocket's haranguing him about the time he spent playing video games, Groot would bet anything that Rocket had the best games of all hidden away on that tablet. Hypocrite.

Groot crept across the floor with his nearly silent steps, until he reached the bin where he'd seen Rocket drop the tablet earlier. Groot reached out with his thin, wooden fingers, and pulled the tablet from its resting place.

Then, he walked back across the cabin just as quietly as before, until he came to his own seat. He plopped down, held the tablet in his hands, and looked at the black screen. Swiping it with his fingers, he saw . . .

. . . nothing.

The screen remained black. Groot scratched the top of his head with one of his long, scrawny, branchlike fingers.

He touched the screen again.

Still nothing.

Maybe it was voice-activated?

"I am Groot?" he whispered.

That didn't work, either.

"I am Groot," he said, and it wasn't an attempt at a password. It was a curse. Rocket wouldn't have approved. Or, maybe he would have.

Groot briefly thought about tricking Rocket into touching the screen, somehow getting him to swipe his furry finger on the tablet screen to see if that would turn it on. But that didn't seem like such a good idea, in that it couldn't possibly work.

So he sat there for a moment, staring at the black screen, thinking. And then he noticed something peculiar. It looked like a corner of the blackness on the screen was . . . peeling? That was decidedly strange. Groot pinched the corner with two fingers, and pulled on it. As he did so, the "black screen" peeled right away, revealing the completely unlocked tablet.

Rocket actually kept his tablet unlocked, and used a decoy screen to hide the fact that it was on?

Groot couldn't believe it. He smiled, and wanted to shout "I am Groot!" but he thought better of it. Instead, he practically raced back to his seat, sat down, and looked at the tablet. What he saw was almost more disappointing than a fully blacked-out screen.

There wasn't a game.

There weren't any games.

There were just a bunch of words.

Ugh. Bummer.

Groot used his finger to flick through pages and pages of text. What was this, some sort of book? He'd never seen Rocket read before.

Suddenly his eye caught on two sentences.

I think he's a tree. He looks like a tree.

Groot paused, thought, leaned in more closely, and attempted to use his finger to make the text bigger. "I am Groot," he whispered to himself. These weren't just any words.

They were *Rocket's* words.

And they seemed to be about Groot.

ENTRY 3X-AFVM.2

I think he's a tree. He looks like a tree.

Let's just say he's a tree.

I liked him right away. He doesn't talk much. Just the three words. Over and over and over. But I've never met anyone who said so much with such a limited vocabulary.

"I am Groot." Who knew it could mean almost anything?

Anyway. I just want to reiterate for future generations who end up reading this, that it ain't a diary. It's a journal. Which is totally different. And I don't think it's even a journal, really. It's more like a place where I put down all my thoughts and all the cool stuff I've done so one day plain dumb people can celebrate me and maybe build me a shrine or somethin', I don't know. I'd take a museum, too.

If Groot saw this, he'd probably say, "I am Groot," and I'd wanna punch him.

That's the blessing and the curse of speaking tree.

"What's that, tree?"

Groot looked up quickly, sliding the tablet against his chest and down his side. "I am Groot," he replied, trying to look innocent.

Thor smiled indulgently. "Well, you don't need to worry, I won't tell the rabbit," he said. "Your secret's safe with me."

Had he seen anything? Could he possibly know what Groot had been up to?

"I am Groot," Groot said, and repeated, a little faster, and in a snottier tone, just in case there was any doubt, "I am Grooooooot."

Thor cocked an eyebrow. "If I didn't know any better, I'd say that you were being belligerent with me."

Busted.

"I am Groot."

"I'll let it go this time," Thor said, returning his attention to the cockpit window and the vast horizons beyond. "But watch your tongue. Do you even have a tongue?"

Groot wondered what a tongue was.

But more important, he wondered why he'd never seen Rocket scribbling in this secret journal-or-whatever-it-was. God knew they'd spent enough time together. It seemed Rocket had been writing in this for at least as long as he and Groot had known each other, if that first entry was any indication. Was Groot really that self-involved that he'd simply never noticed?

"I am Groot," he said to himself, nodding sagely. Yes, yes he was.

A smile spread over Groot's face. Well, he'd found it now, so that was something. He hoped that Rocket would stay busy for a little longer so he could read some more. Maybe he'd find out some really embarrassing pieces of information that he could use to leverage more video game time.

Groot covertly turned his chair as sideways-facing as it would go and peeked at the tablet. He scrolled through some entries at random and started to read.

ENTRY 3X-AFVM.6

This planet is a trash hole. Really. It's just littered with trash. Which makes sense, because it's where most of the planets in this sector dump all their garbage.

Even the planet's name sounds like a trash hole—Glabos.

Who names these planets? People who want to be universally hated?

Glabos.

Gimme a break.

We've been here about an hour, and it's an hour of my life I'll never get back. Groot and I came here because rumor had it there was some big score to be made. Except when we got here—surprise! There was no score.

You wanna know what *was* there? Guess. Go on, I'll wait.

You'll never guess, so I'll tell you. What happened was, we landed our ship, which was a little more stolen than not stolen, if you know what I mean. And no sooner had we left the ship, looked around for our contact who had been rumored to be there, who of course wasn't there, the moron, then we came back to find the ship stripped to its gears.

Groot said, "I am Groot," and he was right. We should have figured that if you land on a garbage planet, you should expect garbage.

Which was exactly what we got.

The ship was toast. We wouldn't be able

to fly it, not without extensive repairs. And it's not like I was gonna put units I didn't have into a ship I didn't own.

So now we gotta find a way off of this ball of sludge. We're gonna go and explore the outpost nearby, and see if they got a bar or something. We could use a drink, and maybe we'll find out something useful.

Or maybe we'll get into a fight. I could use one of those, too.

CHAPTER 3

ENTRY 3X-AFVM.11

Guess what? That fight I was talkin' about earlier? I found it. Oh, and it was a beauty, too. You should see the other guy! I got him right in the eye!

And the other eye.

And the other eye.

And the . . . you get the idea.

The thing had a lotta eyes, is what I'm saying.

The outpost is pretty small, just a few buildings that look like they were built out of whatever scrap metal anyone could find. I asked the bartender about it, and he told me and Groot that this was the garden spot of Glabos.

So there's that.

The bar was packed. In addition to planets dumping their trash on this dump, lots of pilots use Glabos as a kind of quick stop in between jobs when they don't want to be found. I guess because even if someone knew you were on Glabos, they would never in a million years come here on account of how awful the place is.

Can't say as I blame 'em. The smell's really getting to me. And everyone knows I got a highly attuned sense of smell. It's one of my most enviable character traits.

The bartender, I called him Gus, even though that wasn't his name, he said that me and Groot weren't really welcome there. I asked him why not, and he said it was because we looked like the types who wouldn't pay for drinks.

I said that was crazy, but not because he wasn't right. I mean, he was totally right. I had no intention of paying for drinks. But it was crazy of him to say it without him really knowing us.

Anyway, before I could make a big stink about it, Groot put some units down on the counter, because if there's one thing Groot hates it's people makin' assumptions about us, and the bartender got us our drinks. Good ol' Gus.

We sat down at a table, and that's when I noticed the guy with all the eyes. He was just this big, round blob, with all these eyestalks sticking out of it. And then there were the arms and hands. About six of 'em, though Groot said later that he counted at least eight. Personally, I think he was just exaggerating so he could have a story to tell later.

I said, "What, a six-armed guy with a

zillion eyes isn't enough of a story? He's gotta have eight arms now?"

Then he said, "I am Groot," and I knew there was no talking him out of it. For all I know, he's writing his own entry right now, bragging all about it.

Where was I? The big round blobby eye guy, right. So Groot and me, we're sitting there in this dive, minding our own business, when the blobby eye guy comes over to our table. At first, he doesn't say anything. Just stands there, staring at us. Because let's face it, with that many eyes, what else was he gonna do?

Finally, I said, "Why don't you take a picture, it'll last longer."

He still didn't say anything, and I think that's when I realized that was because he didn't have a mouth.

Instead, I heard this voice in my head. As it turned out, the guy was a telepath.

He told me his name was Skoort, and he was looking for me.

Inside my head I asked, "Why?"

Then Skoort thought, "Because I have your ship. Well, parts of it, anyway."

CHAPTER 4

"You're not making any sound back there, and I don't like it."

Groot jumped in his seat and glanced over his shoulder. He saw Rocket in the captain's chair, gazing out into space.

"I am Groot," Groot snarled. He sounded angry, but he was startled—it appeared he'd been out-sneaked by Rocket. How did he know that Groot was up to something? It was like he had eyes in back of his head or something.

Groot sighed a little before saying, "I am Groot" to Rocket in a softer voice.

"It's just when you're quiet, that's when I generally assume that you're up to something," Rocket said back to his friend. "I mean, I figure Thor has good reason to be quiet. He just lost everybody he ever cared about."

Thor looked up at Rocket. The Asgardian's stare looked like it could melt a hole right through his head.

"Sorry I said anything," Rocket mumbled.

Groot shrugged. "I am Groot."

"Oh, yeah, you're *real* sensitive," Rocket said as he adjusted the pod's controls. "Don't give me that."

"I am Groot," Groot sneered, and then turned his attention back to the tablet. Curled up in his chair, holding the tablet close, Groot knew that Rocket would think that he was just playing his games. He couldn't possibly know that he was reading Rocket's journal.

Could he?

ENTRY 3X-AFVM.18
When Skoort said that he had parts of our ship, he wasn't kidding. He reached

one of his six hands inside his globby body, which was just one of the grossest things I've ever seen. Then he rummaged around for a few seconds, until he pulled the hand back out and in it was a master ion tube. Master ion tubes are kinda important, because without 'em, the engine on your ship ain't gonna run too good. Or at all.

Not only was it a master ion tube, but it was *our ship's* master ion tube. I know this, because it was missing the safety. I had taken the safety off the master ion tube so we could get a little extra speed outta the engine. 'Course the downside of doing that is that the engine might explode. But it's the chance you take, y'know?

Anyway. So Skoort's sitting there, rolling MY master ion tube in the palm of one of his slimy hands. And he smiles at me. At least, I *think* he was smiling at me. It was hard to tell, because he didn't really have a mouth, just a series of nose holes that he was breathing through. They curled up, and it sorta looked like a smile, which was extremely creepy.

"Wow. I guess you DO have parts of my ship," I thought inside my head, which is where I like to do my thinking. "Give me one good reason why I shouldn't fry you right now."

"Because if you do, you'll never get the rest of your ship back," Skoort thought back to me. Then he leaned back, and grinned (again, hard to tell) even bigger. I didn't like the guy, but I had to admire his moxie.

"You have my interest, Skoort," I thought to him. And if I'm being truthful, I probably thought a bunch of other things, too, that I wouldn't want to write here because this is for posterity. Maybe I'll add an appendix, though.

"I know why you're here," Skoort thought, and he kept most of his eyes on me, while a few seemed to curl around, like he was keeping a lookout for something. "And I know that your contact is, how shall we say, deceased?"

"Dead?" I said out loud, forgetting for a hot second who I was dealing with. And apparently I said it at a decent enough volume that all heads in the bar turned around to stare right at me.

"What are you lookin' at, jerks?" I yelled.

"I am Groot!" came erupting from beside me, sounding menacing.

"EXACTLY," I said, glad to have my pal backin' me up.

"Please do try to keep your voice down," Skoort thought. "Or don't use it at all, preferably. As I was saying, your contact is dead. A bit of a . . . disagreement over terms, shall we say."

"I bet," I thought to the blob. "So you killed our contact, and now *you're* our new contact. And you took my ship."

"Parts of your ship," Skoort replied.

"Details," I snapped in my head. "I want my ship back before I even discuss the job."

Skoort leaned his blobby body back in the seat, and folded four hands behind what I guess passed for his neck. Then he thought, "Or?"

"Or," I thought, "I let Groot drain the sap outta ya."

Then Skoort looked over at Groot, who was busy pouring a drink into his mouth. He finished it, slammed the mug down, and stared at Skoort. "I am Groot," he said slowly.

"Yes, I believe he would," Skoort thought. "Very well. I'll give you back the master ion tube as a gesture of goodwill."

Then he dropped the slime-covered master ion tube on the table in front of me. It looked really gross.

So I made Groot touch it.

"I am Groot!"

He was protesting. Big baby. I picked it up anyway.

"So what's the score?" I thought, anxious to get the job done, get paid, get my ship back, and get the hell off of Glabos.

"Oh, you'll like it," Skoort thought. "I need you to steal a core."

"Great," I thought. "A core. A core to *what*?"

"Nothing," Skoort said, chuckling, his whole glob of a body shaking up and down. "Just this planet."

"Wait—what now?"

"I am Groot?"

CHAPTER 5

ENTRY 3X-AFVM.19

I didn't know this, but Groot looked it up for us, and it turns out that the main reason everyone dumps all their trash on this garbage hole of a planet is because of its core. Except it's no ordinary core. They call it an endo-thermic core. It's about the size of a marble, and has an internal temperature of about 28 million degrees, give or a take a couple of million degrees.

It's hot, is what I'm saying.

And this endo-thermic core produces so much heat that it can incinerate anything. So some enterprising jerk figured out that it could be used to burn garbage, and they could make a lot of money off it.

That's why the planet Glabos is a big junk heap.

Ya learn something new every day, whether you want to or not.

All Skoort needed was for me an' Groot to sneak into the processing plant where they housed the endo-thermic core, and steal it.

"Out of curiosity," I thought, "how are we supposed to steal something that's twenty-eight million degrees? I mean, I have a feeling if we just picked it up, we'd be—"

"Ashes?" Skoort thought, completing my thought, which was not at all confusing. "Yes, of course you would. But that's why you'll need this." Then he reached another hand inside his gloopy body, and pulled out a small metallic box.

"What is that?" I asked.

"I am Groot," Groot said.

"I know it's a box," I snapped, and I admit it, I was annoyed. "Anyone lookin' at it can see it's a box."

"It's not just a box," Skoort thought. "It's made of omnium."

"Great," I thought. "Which is important because . . . ?"

If you've never seen a multi-eyed guy roll all his eyes at the same time, then you haven't lived. 'Cause that's what Skoort did when I said that, and it was somethin'. "Omnium is the only material capable of containing the heat of the endo-thermic core. The processor in which the endo-thermic core is housed is made of the same material."

"You're just makin' stuff up now," I said out loud, forgetting again who I was talking to in my agitated state. "Right? I mean, this is all kinda hard to believe."

Skoort didn't roll his eyes; he just gave me an angry look. So did a bunch of the customers in the bar.

"Keep. Your voice. Quiet," Skoort thought. "Or someone is going to quiet it for you."

"That a threat?" I thought.

"No," Skoort replied. "It's a fact."

"I am Groot," the tree said, shakin' his head.

"You an' me both," I muttered.

"This 'box,' as you call it, can absorb the omnium core. Just place it alongside the processor, and it will draw the endo-thermic core inside. Then bring it to me. I'll see that your ship is repaired in the meantime, and that payment is waiting," Skoort thought.

I leaned forward in my seat, and took a long pull off my drink. "You drive a hard bargain," I thought to him. "I don't see how me an' Groot have much of a choice here."

"You don't," Skoort thought, rising up from his seat. "But if you do this, you will be rewarded handsomely. And you and your tree friend can leave Glabos as you came, in peace."

That's when I snorted. And I started laughing. Semi-uncontrollably.

Skoort stared at me with all his eyes. "Why do you laugh?" he thought.

"Groot an' me? We don't go anywhere in peace," I thought right back to him.

"I am Groot."

My buddy agreed.

CHAPTER 6

ENTRY 3X-AFVM.23

You woulda thought that something like a processing plant that had something as valuable as an endo-thermic core inside would be more heavily guarded, but you'd be wrong.

It was even more heavily guarded than that.

"How many idiots do they have standin' around this joint?" I asked Groot, who was perched atop the same junk heap I was. We had made our way out of the bar and left the outpost. Once you leave that, the rest is junk. Literal junk. Everywhere you look. It's just heaps of old, used spacecraft, trash, spacecraft full of trash, and more trash.

Skoort had given us the coordinates for the processing plant, and even trusted us to use his own ship to get there. He didn't want to get too close himself, "for professional reasons," which I assume is code for, "I'm a lazy coward." Pretty sure I was right on that one.

Anyway. Me an' Groot made our way through this colossal junkyard once we touched down as close to the coordinates as we could get, and climbed atop a tower of garbage to get a better look. Below us, we could see a series of conveyor belts that all led into the central processing plant, where the endo-thermic core would burn all that trash to oblivion.

I took a look through a pair of binoculars, and then handed them to Groot, who peered through them for a moment, then tossed them into the garbage below us.

So much for those.

"They got guards stationed all around the plant," I whispered to Groot. "Looks to be about fifty of 'em."

"I am Groot," he shot back.

"Really, fifty-two guards? Exactly? How can you tell? You threw the binoculars away without even taking a good look."

"I am Groot."

"Fine, there are fifty-two guards, I don't want to argue with you. I just want to get in there, get the core, and get out. Easiest way in is gonna be the conveyor belts," I said, an' I started to scramble down the garbage heap. "Let's hide ourselves in some of the trash to get through."

"I am Groot."

"What, you're too good to disguise yourself as a piece of junk?"

ENTRY 3X-AFVM.24

The conveyor belt was one of the best-slash-worst ideas I've ever had. It was one of the best, because we were absolutely able to enter the processing plant unnoticed by all those jerks.

It was the worst, because it turned out the conveyor belts took you right into what we found out later was called the melting pit.

And guess what? The melting pit is exactly what you think it is. It's a big pit. And it melts things.

Like us.

Except it didn't. It almost did. I gotta thank Groot for that.

We had hidden ourselves inside the dented hull of an old V-class cruiser, the kind that rich people used to fly when they went on vacation to one of those pleasure planets. There were still a couple of seats attached to the hull, so we hid under those, which I gotta say was easier for me than Groot, because that guy is not exactly what you would call small.

The whole thing still smelled like suntan lotion, which surprisingly activated my gag reflex. I thought it was funny that the stink of rancid garbage didn't make me want to puke, but the first whiff of suntan lotion made me want to chuck my cookies.

Weird, the stuff you think of.

So everything was goin' great, an' we didn't make a sound as we rolled along the conveyor belt, sneakin' right past the guards.

"It's a little hot, isn't it?" I whispered to Groot.

"I am Groot," he said, folded up with his tree-legs almost touching his face, and that's when I noticed that it wasn't just a little hot.

It was a LOT hot.

I knew somethin' was wrong, but we weren't quite inside the processing plant yet. If we bugged out, the guards would have seen us, and we would have had a massive firefight on our hands. Not that I wouldn't have preferred it, but that would have reduced our chances of grabbing the core and getting outta there unnoticed to about zero.

So we just went with it, until we rolled inside the plant. Immediately, as we peered out of the hull's windowpane, we saw where the conveyor belt was taking us.

Right toward the melting pit. Flames shot out of this enormous, gaping furnace at the end of the conveyor belt. The walls had narrowed, and they butted up against the sides of the belt. I thought maybe we could climb off, but no such luck. I got about an inch away from the surface before I felt my hands start to burn.

"This sucks," I said.

"I am Groot."

Boy, was he right.

The flames grew closer. Or more like, we grew closer to the flames.

Either way, we were gonna burn.

CHAPTER 7

ENTRY 3X-AFVM.24.5

I remember saying to Groot that if he had any bright ideas, this would be a good time.

An' I remember him just looking at me and shrugging. At least, I think he was shrugging. It's kinda hard to tell with him. But the more time me an' Groot spend together, the easier it gets figuring out what he means. So in this case, I think he was saying no.

Entirely unhelpful.

So it was up to me.

We rolled along the conveyor belt hidden by that big hunk of metal, sweatin' like a couple of pigs, flames shooting out of the giant furnace. This was just like staring eternal damnation in the face, only hotter.

"I am Groot," he said.

So I said, "I don't like your tone. What, you think I'm not hot? You think I want to die? The answer is yes I am, an' no I don't!"

Things were lookin' pretty grim for us, when a funny thing happened. I mean, it wasn't funny, like "ha-ha" funny. More like, "this is the weirdest thing I ever seen happen" funny.

One second, the conveyor belt was rollin' along, bringing us closer to certain death, an' the next, there was this deafening bang, an' the conveyor belt jerked to a halt. Then thick black smoke started to pour out from everywhere. You couldn't see nothin'!

"We're in luck," I said to Groot. "Something musta gummed up the works of this machine. Now's our chance to bust outta here and grab the endothermic core!"

The smoke was a gift, an' I didn't care who it was from. I was takin' it. We heard the sounds of workers, people scrambling to try to fix whatever had gone wrong with the conveyor belt. We listened for the sound of people comin' closer, and pretty soon I heard somebody right nearby.

I grabbed him by the leg, an' pulled him down. He couldn't see anything in the smoke, until I dragged the guy right over to me an' Groot. You shoulda seen the look on his face! Whatever he was expecting to see, it sure wasn't us.

The guy tried to scream, but Groot knocked him out by clobbering him with one of his big hands. Remind me never to make him mad.

Then we grabbed the heat-resistant gloves off the unconscious guy's hands.

On the back of one hand was a small chip.

"I am Groot!"

"Yeah, I see it," I said. I knew what it was, too. That little chip could grant access to anywhere in the facility. That's how the personnel moved around the processing plant. I put both gloves on, an' me an' Groot raced through the smoke.

We reached the edge of the conveyor belt, and still couldn't see anything. I figured there had to be a ladder somewhere around here, something that the workers used to descend to the conveyor belt.

But where was it?

We didn't have a lot of time. The smoke was already starting to clear, and one of the workers had just discovered the guy we knocked out. There was all sorts of screaming goin' on, and they were workin' themselves up into a lather.

Ugh, people.

The smoke cleared a little more, an' I could just make out the rungs of a ladder on the wall ahead of us, just a couple a' meters away.

"That's where we gotta go, Groot. Get us over there!"

"I am Groot."

"No, I don't have any better ideas."

So Groot leaned over until he was basically level with the floor, extending his arms slightly as he grabbed one of the rungs. Then I jumped on his back and made my way over onto the ladder. An' I started to climb. Groot followed.

Things were lookin' pretty good.

Until they weren't.

CHAPTER 8

ENTRY 3X-AFVM.24.6

When we reached the top of the ladder, the first thing I saw was the barrel end of a blaster.

The guy holding it looked like he had never used a weapon before. He was shaking, his upper lip was trembling, and he was sweating something awful. What a hot mess.

"Look," I said to him in a low, even voice, trying to sound reassuring. "It's like this. We both know I'm gonna knock the weapon out of your hand, and then my buddy's gonna whack you in the head an' you're gonna be unconscious."

"S-stay back!" the guy said, hands shaking. The guy was gonna fire on us accidentally, just from being so scared. What a way to go.

"I'd like to stay back," I said. "Really. I would. But it's not an option. So let's do this the easy way, an'—"

The next thing I knew, a vine snaked right over my shoulder and thumped the scared guy on the head. Hard.

The guy fell down, dropped the weapon, which immediately discharged, the blast just missing my face. The guy had smacked his head on the metal floor, and knocked himself clean out.

"We gotta work on our communication," I said to Groot as I grabbed the weapon off the floor. "You coulda gotten me killed!"

"I am Groot," was all he had to say for himself.

The nerve of this guy.

Still, I gotta admit, Groot's move was

pretty sweet. For a guy that was so big, and took up so much space, he could be so quiet. He didn't say a word, didn't make a sound, just went to work. I'm lucky to have a partner like that.

Don't tell him I said that. It'll go to his head, an' I'll never hear the end of it.

With the latest obstacle out of the way, we ran along a corridor to a control room at the end of the hallway. Based on what Skoort told us, this is where we would find the endo-thermic core. It seemed like all the personnel were busy down by the conveyor belt level, trying to figure out whatever it was that had broken. I don't know how we would have gotten up here if the thing hadn't broken down.

We made it to the control room door, and there was a big panel that said DANGER. "This must be it," I said, an' I opened the door. Sure enough, we saw the endo-thermic core inside. It was just a tiny thing, the size of a marble.

Even from behind three feet of concrete shielding, the endo-thermic core was glowing bright. We had to avert our eyes.

The thing may have been small, but I wasn't about to overlook it. That would be like someone thinkin' I'm Mr. Nice Guy just because I might not be a giant. Big mistake, buddy.

"Now here's the tricky part," I said to Groot. "We gotta find a way to shut the core down, place the doohickey that Skoort gave us right next to it, and absorb it. Then we gotta scram."

"I am Groot."

"Yeah, tell me about it."

ENTRY 3X-AFVM.24.62
You ever have one of those days where everything just seems to go your way, like you can't lose?

I wasn't havin' one of those.

"I am Groot!" was all he could say, over and over.

"I saw you do it with my own two eyes!" I yelled right at him. I was livid. While I had been busy powering down the containment unit so I could access the endo-thermic core, Groot had accidentally pressed a button he shouldn't a' pressed. He claims he didn't, but he clearly did, because if he didn't, the alarm wouldn'ta been goin' off!

"I am Groot," he mumbled.

This guy.

We heard the commotion, and the people yelling, and the footsteps clambering up the metal ladder.

"We need a distraction, Groot. You gotta go blow something up. Fast!"

Groot didn't hesitate. "I am Groot!" he said, an' he ran off, leavin' me to figure out how to extract the endo-thermic core. It came down to flipping a couple of switches, which was easy.

From behind the shielding, the core stopped glowing.

So far, so good.

Then a timer on the control panel in front of me started counting down, from thirty. So there it was. I had thirty seconds to extract the endo-thermic core before it flamed back to life, incinerating me an' everyone within a fifty-mile radius.

I'm just guessin' about the fifty-mile radius part. For dramatic effect, y'know?

I pulled the shield-release lever, and the shield started to raise. Slowly. Sooooooo slowly. Like, it was gonna take forever.

Once the shield raised up about a foot or so, I flung myself onto the ground and squirmed under it.

There was the endo-thermic core. Just sittin' there, dormant. The funny thing about the core chamber is that it wasn't even hot. In fact, it was kinda cold. While the core was depowered, it was just a little ball of metal. Or somethin'.

I pressed the doohickey up against the small glass box that the endo-thermic chamber was resting in. Then I waited. I looked up, an' saw a timer inside the chamber.

21

20

19

Come on, come on . . .

It was taking forever to absorb the core into the doohickey. I started to wonder if this was some kind of setup. Did Skoort send us out here just to kill us?

Then a few things happened all of a sudden, an' all at once.

The doohickey in my hand made a high-pitched "ping" sound. I looked in the glass box, an' the endo-thermic core had disappeared. I got it!

Then there was an enormous explosion that made the other, previous explosion sound like somebody knocked over a garbage can. It was loud, is what I'm sayin'.

That's when I realized that the timer was down to five seconds, an' the metal shielding was sliding back down right along with it!

I threw myself toward the shield and rolled under, just as it slid shut.

On my tail.

You wanna talk about pain? Try havin' a metal wall slam on your tail.

Worst pain there is.

Anyway, I got the endo-thermic core.

"Wrong. I have the endo-thermic core." I heard the voice, and looked around. But I didn't see anybody.

That's when I realized the voice was inside my head.

CHAPTER 9

ENTRY 3X-AFVM.24.63

"Skoort."

I said it in my head so it sounded like I was cursing. Because believe me, inside? I was cursing up a blue streak.

Standing right in front of me on the platform was Skoort. Well, not really standing, on account of he was a big blob thing. He was in front of me, at any rate. And he was using one of his tentacles to hold a weapon, which was pointed right at my head.

"Rocket. I'll take that, if you don't mind." Skoort jiggled the weapon, pointing at the endo-thermic core I held in my hand.

"This wasn't part of the deal," I thought. Right about now, I was wondering where Groot was, and then Skoort started to laugh. At least I think he was laughing. The sound was coming out of his nose holes. Kinda disgusting, actually, because a bunch of snot came with the sound.

Yecch.

"You forget, anything you think, I can hear," Skoort thought. "Groot is temporarily . . . how shall I say? Indisposed."

"Really? And how's that?"

Skoort burbled along the floor, moving a little closer to me, his weapon still aimed straight at my skull. "He's dealing with the security guards below," Skoort thought. "Strangely enough, someone detonated a small explosive that wrecked the conveyor belt. Then there was another explosive that took out the furnace."

Skoort chuckled again. Again, more Skoort snot. Blecch.

What did I do to deserve this?

"I'm confused," I thought to Skoort. "An' I don't like bein' confused. Why hire us to grab the endo-thermic core, if you were gonna sabotage the processing plant and just take it from us anyway?"

"I needed someone to do the heavy lifting," Skoort replied. "You and the tree seemed like the best candidates. You do have a reputation, you know."

"What kinda reputation?" I thought, and I couldn't help but make a couple a' fists, because as far as I was concerned, those were fightin' words.

"I think you know," Skoort thought. "Now, the endo-thermic core. Before I blow your head off and take it from your corpse."

"When you put it like that . . ." I thought.

I handed the endo-thermic core to Skoort. His tentacle touched the containment box, and then he retracted it inside his big glob of a body. I could see the thing, sitting right there in front of me, suspended in slime.

He was so satisfied with himself that he didn't even notice as I shoved the weapon aside, and ran right up another tentacle to the top of what I could only guess was his head.

"WHAT ARE YOU DOING?!?" Skoort, screaming inside my brain.

"What does it look like I'm doin', you jerk?" I thought right back to him, and I just started to claw away. I was determined to get that endo-thermic core back, even if I had to claw my way through the whole of Skoort to get it. That blob started hollering inside my skull somethin' awful. Just really high-pitched, nasally, whiny, like a baby. An' if you know me, you know how I feel about babies.

"GET OFF OF MY STOMACH!" Skoort shouted, and that's when I realized what I thought was the top of his head was really his stomach.

"You got exactly five seconds to drop that endo-thermic core, or I'm gonna give you a permanent stomach-ectomy," I thought.

"THAT'S NOT A THING!" Skoort yelled.

Know-it-all.

"I am Groot!"

I looked up from slashing away at Skoort's stomach to see Groot standing there, with a security guard hanging off of each arm. Before the guards could do anything, Groot slammed his arms together, knocking the two guards right into each other. They went limp, an' Groot tossed them both aside.

"I am Groot," the big guy chortled.

"Yeah, yeah. Now that you're done showin' off, you think you can help me out here?" I yelled over to Groot. He took a couple a' big steps, and he was right next to me.

I directed my thoughts at Skoort. "I'm gonna ask you one more time, an' I'm gonna ask nice. Gimme the endo-thermic core, or there's gonna be Skoort all over the floor."

I'll say this for Skoort. He may be a pain in the behind, but he's not stupid. His body started to shake and jiggle, and a second later, the endo-thermic core came spewing out one of his nose holes, covered in Skoort slime. The thing fell right into my waiting hand.

SCHLORP.

Yecch.

"Now we want our units, and our ship," I thought to him.

"Your units and— ARE YOU OUT OF OUR MIND?!?" Skoort yelled inside my head. "I don't even have the endothermic core now!"

"Units and ship, or—"

I pointed to Groot, and he made a gesture like he was gonna poke Skoort. Then he mimed all the stuff inside a' Skoort just sorta oozing out all over the floor. "I am Grooooooooot," he said, in a singsong kinda voice, like he was imitating the oozing.

Skoort didn't think anything for a hot second. Then he reached a tentacle inside his body and pulled out a tablet. He swiped the tentacle on the screen a few times.

"There," Skoort thought. "The agreed-upon units have been transferred. And you'll find your ship in full repair at the dock."

"Good call," I thought to Skoort. I looked him in the eye and the eye and the eye and the eye and you get the point. Then I noticed somethin' I didn't before.

"That eye there," I thought. "Artificial?"

Skoort didn't know how to respond. "Y-yes," he stuttered. "Why do you ask?"

"Tell you what," I thought. "You give me the eye, an' I won't tell the whole galaxy that you're a dirty double-crosser."

They say it's best not to kick a guy when he's down, but I think that's the best time to kick 'em, 'cause you know they're not goin' anywhere.

Without even so much as a whisper of an argument, Skoort disengaged the robotic eye from its stalk, and tentacled it to me.

I gave it a look, and then thought,

"Pleasure doin' business with ya, Skoort. May it never happen again."

Groot an' I raced out of the processing plant, an' I heard Skoort's voice in my head say, "The feeling is mutual."

CHAPTER 10

"Maybe you wanna put that thing down and try helpin' out around here?"

Groot's eyes were immediately drawn to Rocket. He saw the mighty pilot and commander of the mission to Nidavellir slowly stretch has arms upward, sit up, then tousle the fur on his head with his right hand.

Groot quickly shoved the tablet underneath a medical pack resting nearby.

"I am Groot," he said in reply. "I am Groot."

"Yeah, you're probably right," Rocket yawned, standing up. "If you did help, I would probably yell at you for helpin' wrong. Ya can't win, can ya?"

"I am Groot."

For a moment, Groot felt a little guilty. It was one thing to sneak on to Rocket's tablet and play games. But reading his friend's secret journal? Without permission?

That was something else entirely.

But at the same time . . . Wow, that story! It was almost better than a video game.

Almost.

"What about you, Thor?" Rocket asked. "You've been pretty quiet."

"Just thinking," the Asgardian replied.

Rocket shook his head. "Yeah, that'll get you in trouble right there. Thinking. I don't recommend it." Changing the subject, Rocket gestured at their surroundings. "Sorry about the accommodations. Aren't you like a king or somethin'? Probably used to travelin' in a big golden chariot."

Thor laughed. "Hardly. You'd be surprised what I'm used to traveling in. And who I'm used to traveling with."

"I am Groot."

Rocket looked over his shoulder and saw

Groot looking out the cockpit window. "What? Suddenly you're some kinda language guru now?" Rocket said.

"Did . . . did you just correct my grammar, tree?" Thor asked, genuinely curious.

"Yeah," Rocket said, scratching the back of his neck. "He said *you* shoulda said, 'And with whom I'm used to traveling.' Said it sounds more kingly."

"Grammar wasn't my best subject in school," Thor admitted. "Hammers 101 was my subject."

"Time well spent. Awright. Where are we now?" Rocket asked, getting down to business.

Thor leaned over to look at one of the ship's data screens. "At our current speed, we should make Nidavellir in roughly three hours, Captain."

Rocket turned his head to look directly at Thor. Then he narrowed his eyes, looking over the bridge of his muzzle. "You makin' fun a' me?"

The Asgardian appeared indignant. "No," he

said. "You're the captain of this vessel, right?"

Rocket seemed to think about that for a few seconds. "Yeah, yeah I am," he replied. Then he turned to face Groot. "An' don't you forget it!"

"I am Groot."

"The mouth on this one," Rocket said, jabbing a thumb in Groot's direction. "I'm gonna go search out some grub from this dump," Rocket said, leaving his seat in the cockpit.

Groot moved into the pilot's seat and plopped down, resting his large feet on a console and tucking his twig-like limbs behind his head. All that reading had made him tired— maybe getting some shut-eye was a good idea.

Suddenly an alarm blared.

Groot's eyes flew open as he rocketed out of the chair, and he panicked for a moment, thinking maybe he had touched something he wasn't supposed to touch. But everything looked intact.

Instantly, Rocket raced back to the console. "What did you just do?" he yelled at Groot.

"I know you pressed somethin' with those big feet a' yours!"

"I am Groot!" the tree creature protested.

"We'll discuss this later," Rocket said. "After I figure out what's wrong."

"You mean you don't know?" Thor asked, concern in his voice.

"All I know is an alarm bell's ringing up here, which means something's wrong down there," Rocket gritted out, pointing at the deck below their feet.

Rocket ran over to a metal panel on the wall that had three protruding levers sticking out from a slot on its left side. He shoved the levers from their bottom locked position to the top, and there was a brief hissing sound as a puff of gaseous coolant leaked into the cockpit. Rocket removed the panel and climbed inside the hole he had opened.

"I'm gonna go fix this crate," Rocket said. He glared at Groot as he put one foot through the hole. "An' when I get back, we're havin' words!"

"I am Groot" was all Groot could manage as Rocket disappeared inside the hatch.

Groot fumed in silence. Why was Rocket always so quick to blame him when things went wrong? Why didn't he believe Groot when he said things weren't his fault?

"I wouldn't worry about it, tree," Thor spoke up, as though reading Groot's mind. "I know his kind. He just needs to blow off some steam, and when he comes back, things will be fine."

"I am Groot," Groot answered despondently.

"Yes, or not."

Thor turned away from Groot, and walked to the console near the pilot's station. The alarm was still blaring.

"How's that?" Rocket yelled, from the narrow access compartment below the deck.

"What am I supposed to be looking for?" Thor asked.

"The alarm to shut off, what else!" Rocket hollered back.

The alarm only seemed to get louder.

"Somehow, I think you've made it worse," Thor called out. "Are you sure you know what you're doing?"

"You're all a bunch of ingrates," Rocket yelled, followed by some unintelligible sounds that Groot assumed was a string of curses.

With Thor and Rocket focused on making the repair, Groot snuck back to his seat, and lifted the tablet out from underneath the med kit, the screen welcoming him back into its world with a soft, inviting glow. Suddenly he didn't feel so bad about going through his friend's things.

"I am Groot," he said belligerently, and he started to read.

CHAPTER 11

ENTRY 3X-AFVN.12.4

We had a little scrape a while ago, me an' the Guardians, with this thing called the Van'Lan. Basically, it was like a giant space amoeba made up of a lot of little space amoebas. The thing nearly destroyed the *Milano* and killed all of us. But as usual, me, Groot, Drax, Gamora, an' Quill made it out in one piece.

The *Milano* wasn't so lucky. The fight against the Van'Lan had drained the ship of all power, and it was just a big, useless hunk of space trash.

We woulda floated there forever, until

life support gave out and we all turned into little Guardian icicles, except we got picked up by the Nova Corps.

I guess that's one of the advantages of no longer being wanted criminals. Once we literally SAVED THE GALAXY from Ronan, we were absolved of any and all crimes by the Xandarians.

Not that I'm admitting to any crimes, in case anyone ever reads this.

Anyway. The Nova Corps towed the *Milano* to the Tradepost, this artificial planet where they can repair ships, weapons, anything, you name it. While the mechanics went to work on the craft, me an' the team decided to kill a few hours by finding the nearest watering hole.

Then we ran into this guy, Rhomann Dey. He's one of the Nova Corps. Met him before. He's all right, I guess.

Dey was luggin' some weirdo in a

long coat along, like he was a prisoner or somethin'.

"Hey, who's your friend here?" Quill asked.

"I am your death, Peter Quill!" the guy yelled.

What a tool.

"This guy is a problem, is who he is," Dey said, picking the jerk up by the collar of his coat and slamming him back down to the ground. "He stole my ship! Can you believe it? Took it for a little joyride. Apparently had a little problem out in space. Someone took a shot at him, knocked out the engine. We brought him in same time we got you."

I figured that was that, an' turned around to head to the bar.

But not Quill. No, Quill had to keep yappin'.

"I'm curious, though," Quill said. "Why are you my death?"

I wanted to scream, "WHO CARES WHY HE'S YOUR DEATH? LET'S GET A DRINK!" but I didn't 'cause I got manners.

The weird guy in the coat went on to talk about this one time when we were at the Boot of Jemiah, this bar on Knowhere, which is a planet blah blah blah whatever. Apparently, me an' Drax had some kinda argument or somethin', and it upset the Orloni races. The Orloni are these little rodents, an' people race 'em against these reptiles called F'Saki. Apparently, a lot of units were at stake, and this jerk bet the most.

"You and your idiot friends interrupted the Orloni races with your ridiculous quarreling!" the guy was yelling. "I was winning! I could have won! I lost all my units!"

"Wait," Quill said. "So you were going to kill us . . ."

"Yes!" the weirdo shouted.

". . . because you lost units . . ."

"Yes!"

". . . on a game?"

"I tried to kill you! I was *this close* to blowing you out of the stars!"

"This has been the weirdest day," Quill said.

We watched as Dey took the guy in the coat away, an' didn't give it another thought.

ENTRY 3X-AFVN.12.6

I was sittin' at the bar, mindin' my own business, with Drax, an' I was happy.

"Do you think we really ruined that man's life?" Drax asked.

I couldn't believe that Drax was gettin' all philosophical on me. Why would he do that? Here we were drinkin' and relaxin', and he had to go and ruin it.

So I waved my hand and said, "Eh, who cares. He tried to ruin our lives. Does anyone care about that?"

"I care," Drax said, taking a drink. "I care very much when someone tries to hurt my friends."

"Oh boy, here we go," I said, because I knew what was comin' next. Drax was gonna get all maudlin on me, an' start goin' on about how the Guardians are his family now, an' we're all he's got, an' then I'm gonna start cryin' but I can't show anyone that I'm cryin', an' WHO NEEDS IT?

Lucky for me, that's when Rhomann Dey reappeared, and set himself down in the seat next to mine.

"We meet again—hey, hey, Rhomann Dey!" I said. "That rhymes."

"Good one," Dey said. "No one's ever said that before." He held up his hand, and motioned for the bartender to sling him a drink.

"Really?" I asked, falling for it.

"No," Dey said. "Everyone says that. They always think they're the first. It's profoundly tiresome."

The bartender put a glass in front of Dey, and poured him a half glass full of some deep amber liquid. Clearly this wasn't Dey's first visit here—when a bartender knows a man's order by heart, that's the kinda thing that impresses me. Not that I was gonna show it.

"So what brings you here?" I asked, a little more belligerent than I needed to be. "We do anything wrong?"

Dey laughed. "Not that I'm aware of. My prisoner's being processed, and I need to hang around here for a while. I thought I'd spend some time with you fine people."

I did a double take.

"Us?" I asked.

Dey nodded.

CHAPTER 12

ENTRY 3X-AFVN.12.8

If you hang around Rhomann Dey long enough, you learn two things:

He pays for drinks.

He's a decent guy.

An' I'm not just sayin' that because he pays for drinks. He's really okay. For Nova Corps.

This is also why my theory—that guys whose bartenders know their drink orders by heart are worth a second glance—holds up.

"I'm curious," Dey said to me, taking a sip from his glass. "How did you get hooked up with Quill, anyway?"

"Don't you know this already?" I said. "Didn't you arrest all of us? What, are you losin' your memory or somethin'?"

"No, I know the story," Dey said. "I just like hearing it, is all."

It wasn't much of a story, actually. Me an' Groot were on Xandar, lookin' to fetch a bounty on Quill. He had stolen this thing called the Orb from the Ravagers on the planet Morag. By doing that, he crossed Yondu Udonta, who put a bounty on Quill's head. We needed the units, so me an' Groot figured we would grab Quill when he tried to sell it on Xandar.

The plan kinda worked, sorta, in the sense that we did catch Quill. Until we didn't, and then we were caught by the Nova Corps. Then we got thrown into the Kyln prison facility with Quill and Gamora, where we met Drax and all teamed up to bust out of the prison and blah blah blah you know the rest.

"Why are you askin' so many questions, anyway?" I said. "Doesn't anybody talk to you?"

Dey laughed, took a gulp from his glass, and set it down on the table. "Look, I'm gonna tell you something that Quill doesn't know. No one else knows. And I'm gonna trust that you're not gonna tell anyone, even after you've left the Tradepost."

Suddenly this conversation got a whole lot more interesting.

I leaned in, my face hovering just over my glass, real dramatic like. "This is about the guy who wanted Quill dead, right?"

Dey nodded.

"Y'know, I'm not really known for my ability to keep my mouth shut," I said. "Some people have even called me a loudmouth. Of course, those people end up unconscious."

"I'm telling you," Dey said, looking

around. It was like he was making sure that no one was listening or somethin', "precisely *because* you're a loudmouth."

"That makes no sense," I said.

Dey leaned in a little closer. "I guess what I'm trying to say is, because you talk so much, no one will believe you. And also, if you tell anyone, I'll hunt you down and take you right back to the Kyln."

"Yer bluffin'," I said, lookin' Dey straight in the eye.

"Maybe," Dey said, smiling. "There's only one way to find out."

I took a long pull from my glass, then wiped my mouth with the back of my hand. "So are you gonna tell me or what?"

"That guy," Dey said, his voice really quiet now, "his name is Meer Kaal."

"Uh-huh," I said, pretending like the name meant something to me, which it didn't.

"He's Kree."

"Uh-huh," I repeated.

"You're . . . you're not getting it, are you?" Dey said.

"Getting what?"

Dey sighed. "You think Meer Kaal just decided all on his own to 'get revenge' on Quill for the incident back on Knowhere?" he said.

"To be honest, I did," I replied. "But the way you just said that makes me think that he didn't."

"No, he didn't. Kaal's part of a Kree splinter group. And let's just say they're not happy that the Kree are no longer at war with Xandar."

"I'm waiting for the part where this all makes sense," I said. I really was. My head was startin' to hurt and, as much as I was enjoyin' Dey's company, I kinda wanted to go somewhere and sleep for a few hours. Drax had wandered off a little while ago after he'd gotten all weepy on us, and it was just me and Dey left.

"Kaal's sister was some kind of big-shot scientist back in the day of the Kree-Xandar War," Dey jabbered. "Supposedly, she hid a stash of weapons, and this Kree splinter group would love to get their hands on them."

"And let me guess," I said, because I'm a good guesser. "They're stashed somewhere at the Tradepost."

"No," Dey said, lookin' at me kinda funny. "That would just be way too coincidental. Life doesn't work that way, pal."

I shrugged. "Guess not."

"We do think that Meer Kaal knows where the stash is hidden. But he's not talking to us. So I thought maybe, someone with your particular . . . talents . . . might be able to persuade him to give up the information."

And there it was. I couldn't believe it. A Nova wanted my help.

I started laughin'.

"What's so funny?" Dey asked as my laughter got louder an' louder. People in the bar started lookin', and one guy even started laughin' along with me. Of course I stopped laughin' then and glared at the moron, because don't start laughin' like a crazy person if you don't know what you're laughin' about. That's called being an idiot.

"For a second there, I thought you were askin' for my help!" I said.

"Yeah, that's exactly what I'm doing," Dey said. "Don't be a jerk, okay?"

"Hey, hey, I'm sorry," I said, because I could see that Dey was really serious. "But . . . why me?"

"It's because you're you," Dey replied.

"What's that supposed ta mean?"

"Don't take offense, it's not an insult," Dey said. "I just mean that I'm with the Nova Corps. We have rules. You're with the 'Guardians of the Galaxy.' I don't think you guys really have rules."

"Gotcha," I said, and then I leaned back in my chair. I didn't say anything for a little bit. Just sat there, staring at Dey.

"Are you gonna say something?" Dey asked, looking mildly uncomfortable. "Because if you're just gonna stare at me, it's kinda creepy now. Is that what you're going for?"

"What's in it for me?" I asked, because that's the kinda thing you gotta ask when someone asks you to do somethin' like this.

"As a Guardian of the Galaxy, shouldn't you be doing this just to help out the citizens of the universe?"

It was a good thing for him that I didn't have a drink in my mouth, or Dey woulda been wearing it. Still, I'm sure he could tell by the look that I gave him that the whole "do it for the good of the galaxy" wasn't gonna cut it for me.

"Fine," Dey said with an exasperated sigh. "What do you want?"

I thought about this one long an' hard. What did I want? An' I'll admit it, even though I liked Dey, it felt nice to be in a position of power for once over a Nova. A plan began to take shape—wouldn't be the worst thing to bring a Nova down a peg or two, even a nice Nova like Dey. Show them the other side to the kinds of people they were always lookin' down on and arrestin' and all that.

"I want you to go with me."

Dey just stared at me for a beat.

"I can't go with you," he said at last, enunciating every word like I was someone he had to talk slow to. "That kind of defeats the whole purpose of me asking you to do this in the first place."

"That's my offer," I said. "Take it or leave it."

"This is really insane, you know this,"

Dey said, shaking his head. He stood up from the table, looked at me, then turned and walked away. I watched him as he moved past a buncha creeps who were just hangin' out by the entrance, and Dey walked outside.

I took a long sip from my drink.

Wait for it, wait for it . . .

Dey came back through the door, and walked right over.

"You win," he said. "But this is a terrible idea."

Hah! I knew it. They always come crawlin' back.

"Aren't they all?" I said, an' we were off.

CHAPTER 13

ENTRY 3X-AFVN.12.95

We weren't even a minute from the bar when we ran right into him.

I mean, literally. I ran right into him.

It was like hitting a wall, and it hurt.

In the middle of the street, I stood there, rubbing my nose. "Why don't you watch where you're goin', ya big ape?" I said.

Drax stared at me, and turned his head. Guess he hadn't wandered off that far. "I always watch where I'm going. I can't help it. My eyes will only let me see this way." Then he pointed forward.

"So freakin' literal," I said, still rubbing my snout.

"Rhomann Dey," Drax said, clearly surprised to see the two of us exiting the bar together. "What are you still doing with Rocket?"

"Nothing," he said, an' he looked really uncomfortable sayin' it. "Why would I be doing anything with Rocket? We're not *doing* anything. Exactly the opposite."

Dey was a terrible liar. Luckily, if there was one person who was gonna believe this, it was Drax.

"I don't know why you would be doing anything with him," Drax said. "That's why I asked."

I figured I should jump in an' save Dey some distress, before his head exploded or something. "Dey's helpin' me get some parts for the *Milano*," I said easily.

"I thought the repairs were almost done," Drax said, looking confused. "I just came from the repair station."

"Yeah, well, there's some stuff they don't know about, awright?" I said. "Look, why don't you go back in the bar, settle in, get yourself another drink. I'll be there in a few."

Drax stared at Dey, an' then he looked at me. I gotta be honest. For a second there, I wasn't sure whether or not he was buyin' it.

"A few what?" Drax asked finally.

"A few minutes. What else would it be?"

"I don't know," Drax said.

"That's why I asked," we both said.

An' with that, Drax kept on walkin', leavin' me an' Dey to our business.

"That was close," Dey said.

"Whaddaya mean, 'That was close'? So what if Drax knew what we were doin'? He wouldn't care," I told him.

"Maybe he wouldn't, but I would," Dey said. "What I'm doing is highly against procedure and proper protocol. If word of this gets out—"

"Lemme guess." I cut him off before the guy could get any more self-righteous. "If word of this gets out, you can kiss your job good-bye, an' they'll throw you in that floating space prison along with all the criminals you busted. Sound about right?"

Dey was quiet, and then he just started to nod. Slow at first, then faster an' faster. "Yeah, that's exactly right," he said. "So you see why I'm real anxious not to have that happen."

"I get the picture," I told him. An' I did. Like I said before, Dey was a decent guy, an' while I was definitely enjoyin' this little power trip I was on, I didn't have any desire to see him get into trouble.

I mean, more trouble than we were going to get into.

The street was wet, on account of it

had been raining since we stepped outside the bar. The rain on the Tradepost
was this weird purple color. Somethin' to
do with all the pollution that's pumped
out of all the repair facilities on this
artificial planet. Junk goes up into the
air, purple rain comes down.

Also, it stings a little when it hits your
skin, but I'm sure that's fine.

We started off down the street again,
passing by a buncha repair shops. When
we reached the end of the street, Dey
pointed up a long, winding road.

"Why are you pointing like that?" I
asked.

"The place where Meer Kaal's being
held," Dey said. "It's that way."

"How far that way?"

"Like . . ." Dey stopped talking, an'
then he held his hands up, just a few
inches apart. "This far?"

"Really? This far," I said, and mim-
icked his hands with mine. "If he was

'this far,' we'd be standin' on top of him. No, really, how far is it?"

"Eighteen kilometers," he said, completely matter-of-fact.

"An' we were just gonna walk?" I was shakin' my head at this point, an' gettin' ready to turn around and head back to the bar to meet Drax.

"We need to keep a low profile," Dey said. "They can't know we're coming."

"Relax," I said. "I got an idea."

ENTRY 3X-AFVN.12.958

"So your idea was stealing a vehicle?"

Dey was sittin' to my left, an' I had put the hovercar into fifth gear. The thing had a lot of power, I gotta admit. We were doin' about 200 kilometers an hour, so we'd be there in no time. Way better than *walking*.

Now, strictly speaking, the hovercar was, in fact, stolen. That's because I stole it. But I wasn't so much stealing it as I was borrowing it without asking. An' how could I ask? The repair shop was closed, no one was there. Even when I broke in, I still couldn't find anyone to ask. So I figured I could just take it, use it for a half hour or so, then return it before anyone was the wiser.

"Yeah," I said to Dey.

"I can't believe I'm going along with this," he muttered.

That made me laugh. "I can't believe you're goin' along with it, either," I said right back to him. "Can you imagine what kinda trouble you'd be in if they found out you were stealin' vehicles on the Tradepost?"

Dey just shook his head at me.

The rest of the ride was pretty quiet except for the sound of the hovercar's engines.

CHAPTER 14

"What about now? What's happening now?" Rocket yelled from the hatch.

Thor stood at the pilot's station, looking at the controls. "The alarm is no longer blaring that foul noise," he said. "The flashing red light tells another story, however."

"What flashing red light?" Rocket hollered.

"The one that says 'warning,'" Thor shouted right back.

Groot was basically oblivious to this entire exchange, sequestered away in his own personal space, back to the cold hull, pilfered tablet in hand. Where had he been while this whole adventure between Rocket and Dey had occurred? Probably doing something boring, like sleeping.

He looked up for a second when he heard the word *warning*, then promptly returned to the tablet.

"Is it blinking fast or blinking slow?"

"It's blinking rather quickly," Thor said, his brow furrowed.

"Well, that ain't good," Rocket said.

ENTRY 3X-AFVN.13.10

We had to ditch the hovercar about a half kilometer away from the place where they were holding Meer Kaal. Any closer, an' they woulda heard us coming. Turns out the mechanics at the repair shop hadn't gotten around to fixin' this one yet. It was makin' a real racket.

"You couldn't have stolen a working hovercar?" Dey asked.

"You're welcome, Rocket," I said sarcastically. As if he'd had any better ideas!

The landscape on the Tradepost was weird, because it was kinda like a real planet, but kinda not. There were plants, but only because they had grown around the metal structure of the world over decades. There were some real trees, but mostly there were antenna relays all over the place. They looked like trees, sort of, if you squinted. So we hid the hovercar behind a bunch of relays, and figured we'd hope for the best.

Up ahead, there was a big hill, an' at the top of the hill, there was a metal building maybe a couple a' floors tall.

"That's it," Dey said, pointing.

"You sure like to point, don't you?"

Dey didn't bother saying anything to that. He raised his eyebrows, an' said, "Meer Kaal is in there. Now, there's only one Nova guarding him right now, right outside the holding cell."

"Just one guy? Really? Why don't you have more people guarding him?" I asked. "I mean, if he holds the key to you guys getting your hands on this weapons cache, why wouldn't you have a whole platoon here?"

"Well, we're trying not to attract a lot of attention," Dey said. "Plus, the holding cell has no windows, and only one door. It's not like he's going anywhere. And this is just temporary. He's scheduled for pickup within an hour. So this is your window."

"*Our* window," I reminded him.

"So what's the plan?" Dey asked, ignoring me.

"The plan?" I said. Truth was, I didn't have a plan. I was makin' everything up. "You go up an' ask to check on the prisoner. I'll handle it from there."

"You're not gonna do anything bad, are you?" Dey asked.

"Who, me?" I said, the picture of innocence.

ENTRY 3X-AFVN.13.11

I was standing right behind a bunch a' relays, pretty sure that no one could see me. The building where they were holding Meer Kaal was just ahead. An' I could hear Rhomann Dey, who had approached the holding cell.

"Denarian Dey," the Nova in charge of the prisoner said. "We weren't expecting you."

Sheesh. Did all these guys call each other by their full names all the time? What a bunch a pretentious idiots.

"I'm here to check on the prisoner before the transfer," Dey said. "I have a list of security procedures. I need to review them with you." I heard Dey's retreating footsteps, followed by the Nova officer.

That was my cue.

I bolted from my hiding spot, and covered the distance between the relays an' the holding cell in no time flat. I couldn't see inside, because there were no windows. But that was okay. I didn't need to be able to see inside in order to break in. I had everything I needed right in my hand.

It was a rotating laser saw, somethin' I swiped back at the repair shop. Figured it would come in handy, an' I figured right.

It was magnetic, so it attached right to the wall. I set the radius to make a hole just big enough for me to squeeze through. Then I pressed the button and voilà. The tiny saw started to move in a circle, its laser cutting right through the metal beneath it. A few seconds later, the saw finished the circumference, and had sliced a hole in the metal wall.

An' yes, in case yer wonderin', I set the angle so the metal circle I cut out fell toward me, an' not into the cell where it would make a big racket.

I'm not a complete reject.

ENTRY 3X-AFVN.13.12

This Meer Kaal guy. What a piece a' work.

I wasn't inside the cell for a hot second before he was all over me. Not like he was attackin' me or anythin'. I just mean he was hysterical is all.

"Who sent you?" he screamed in my face. His hands were bound together in front of him by a set of cuffs, and his ankles were bound, too. He was up in my face, an' I didn't like it.

So I drop-kicked him right in the chest.

He went down on the floor, an' I'd be lyin' if I said the sound of it didn't make me happy.

"You're going to kill me!" Kaal shouted.

I'd had enough, so I covered his mouth with my hands.

"I'm not gonna kill you," I said in the quiet voice I save for morons who are really startin' to get on my last nerve. "I'd like to, an' if you keep yappin' like this, I probably will later. If you so much as raise your voice above a whisper again? I'll bite ya."

That quieted him down a little. But then I had to add a little somethin' I just couldn't resist.

"I got space rabies."

Meer Kaal's eyes got really big at that one. Groot woulda been proud a me. I didn't laugh or nothin'. Just kept the straightest face I could.

Then I pulled my hand away from

Meer Kaal's mouth. He didn't scream again, just like I figured he wouldn't.

"You wanna know who sent me?" I said.

Meer Kaal nodded.

"Thanos," I said.

I'm not certain, but I think it's possible the poor guy mighta wet his pants.

CHAPTER 15

ENTRY 3X-AFVN.13.13

"The weapons stash. Where is it?"

"I don't know what you're talking about."

An' I thought Rhomann Dey was a lousy liar. This guy was the worst. His eyes were twitching, his lip was trembling, an' he was sweating like Quill does when he gets really nervous. I wish Groot was here to see this. He woulda gotten a kick out of it.

After what happened . . . after the thing with Ronan, an' Groot giving his life for all of us? I just . . . I don't know what I woulda done if we didn't have the little sap come back to us.

I know he's not the same. But that doesn't matter.

We still have him, even if he's different. We're lucky to have him.

I'm lucky to have him. It's like having a second chance.

Holy crust, look at me gettin' all sappy. No pun intended.

Anyway, this jerk was this close to tellin' me everything I wanted to know. You wanna know how I knew? I mean, other than the wettin'-his-pants thing from before.

He was startin' to mumble.

They're always ready to talk when they start ta mumble.

"Look, there's two things that both of us know for sure," I said as I shoved him onto his back. I jumped on top of his chest, an' I started to pace back an' forth right in front of his face. "I know you're lying, and you know you're lying."

He mumbled somethin', I couldn't understand it. So I grabbed his cheeks and shoved my face right into his.

"What was that?" I said. "I'm feelin' a little bitey."

When I was up close an' holdin' him by his face, I noticed somethin' weird. Somethin' about his right ear. Then it hit me. It was a prosthetic ear.

As soon as I knew what it was, I decided it was gonna be mine.

"I said that I don't know where the weapons are," Meer Kaal chirped, like a bird. "Not exactly."

"Not exactly?" I said, letting go of his cheeks, makin' sure I left a couple a' claw marks for effect. "A minute ago, it was, 'I don't know anything,' and suddenly you know somethin', but not exactly somethin'."

I started to pace on his chest again. "So where is 'not exactly,' exactly?"

The guy started mumbling again, an' I was gettin' tired of it. Then I heard a commotion coming from outside. I jumped off Meer Kaal, an' ran over to the door of the holding cell. It was locked, naturally, an' there was no window, so it wasn't like I could see out—then again, no one could see in.

But I could *hear* out just fine.

"Are you certain?"

It was the other guard.

"I'm certain," Dey said. "You've done the whole lockdown wrong. We're going to need to review all the codes. Right. Now."

"Sir, yes sir!" the guard said.

I had to hand it to Dey. He really had the guy going!

Since it sounded like Dey had everything under control, I turned my attention back to the mumbler.

"Tell me a story," I snapped, "an' make it a good one."

"The weapons you're looking for," he said, mouth twitching, "won't do you any good, even if you had them!"

"Let me be the judge a' that," I said. Then I snapped my mouth shut.

Meer Kaal flinched.

"They'll kill me," he said. "If they find out I told you, told anyone, they'll kill me!"

"An' what do you think I'll do if you *don't* tell me?" I said, baring my teeth to remind him. That was a good line. Turned out I was really good at this!

Kaal gulped, an' looked at me like he was weighing his options. I guess he decided that the danger in front of him was worse, because he said, "The weapons are on Aphos Prime."

"Aphos Prime?" I said. "That sounds made up." I said *that* because it *did* sound made up.

"It's not, I swear," Meer Kaal said. "You can ask anyone."

"I'm not askin' anyone," I said, gettin' up in the guy's face again. "I'm askin' you."

He gulped. "Aphos Prime is real. I can give you the coordinates," he said.

I pulled this very tablet from a pouch on my side. I swiped it on, opened the navigation program, and handed it to him.

"Put 'em in," I ordered.

He took the tablet, and started to type. Then he gave the tablet back to me. I looked at the screen.

"This for real?" I said, droppin' the tough-guy act for just a second.

"It's for real," he gasped. "I swear. Now that I've told you, my life is worthless."

"I got news for ya, pal," I said. "Your life was worthless before you told me."

The guy looked like he was gonna cry. I couldn't stand it. I started laughin'.

"Look, I'm just messin' with ya. You're in the custody of the Nova Corps. These guys are top-notch. Don't worry, nobody's gonna get to you."

"You got to me," he said.

"Yeah," I replied. "But I ain't nobody."

I shoved the tablet back into the pouch an' headed toward the hole in the wall. Before I left, I turned around, an' looked at Meer Kaal.

"Now, if I was you, I wouldn't mention that I was ever here," I said. "Because if you do, then I'm gonna have to come back, and then we all know what I'm gonna do, right?" I made a mock chomping noise with my mouth, for added dramatic effect.

Meer Kaal didn't say anything, he just sorta looked at me, an' I could see the fear in his eyes.

Under his breath, I heard him mumble the words.

"Space rabies."

"That's right," I said. Then I ran over to him, which surprised the stuffing right outta him.

An' you'll never guess what I did next.

CHAPTER 16

ENTRY 3X-AFVN.13.20

"You shook your *butt*?"

I coulda sworn that's what Rhomann Dey said, but it was hard to hear him over the sound of the hovercar's engine.

"What?" I shouted.

"I said, you took his *what*?"

Oh. That made a lot more sense than the other thing.

I started laughin'. "I took his ear," I said.

Then it was Dey's turn to look at me funny. "You took his rear?"

"No, his ear, not his rear," I yelled

over the din. "Geez, get your hearing checked."

We were speeding down the hill, and we were both feelin' pretty good. I had the information Dey wanted from Meer Kaal. I went back through the hole, then me and Dey beat it back to the spot where we'd hidden the hovercar. Surprisingly, it was right where we left it. Usually my luck runs the other way. Even more surprisingly, the hovercar started up right away even though it was a hunka junk.

"What are you gonna do with a prosthetic ear?" Dey asked in disbelief.

He had a point. I really didn't need it. But I wanted it. You know who would understand? Groot would understand. Call it a flaw in my character. I mean, I wouldn't call it a flaw, but I'm sure there are some who would. And they'd be wrong. Yeah, Groot would understand.

"So what did you find out from Meer Kaal?" Dey asked.

That's when the engine dropped out of the hovercar.

Literally. It just dropped right out from the bottom, and we went skidding off what passed for a road and right into a big honkin' metal antenna. We slammed into it like a bug on a windshield.

My back was killin' me when I crawled out of the hovercar. I looked around for Dey, but didn't see him anywhere.

"Dey!" I shouted as I limped away from the wreck. "Where are you? You didn't die on me, did you?"

Seriously. What a ridiculous way to go.

"Over here," he said. I heard his voice comin' from over a metal ridge that looked like it was made out of the rusted-out hull of a Xandarian ship. I climbed through a big hole, and saw Dey there. He was sitting up, rubbing his head, and turning his neck back and forth.

"What are you doin' all the way over here?" I asked.

"What does it look like, Rocket?" he said, an' I detected a note of sarcasm in his voice that I didn't particularly like.

It kind of made me feel bad. Like maybe I shouldn'ta been pokin' fun at him in this instance.

What was goin' on? What was this? Me, suddenly givin' a flippin' care about someone else?

Ugh, this day was never gonna end.

"Groot!" Rocket's voice thundered from the underbelly of the hole, jolting Groot out of his trancelike state as he read through Rocket's journal entries.

"I am Groot," the treelike creature called back, quickly slipping the tablet underneath the med pack.

"I don't wanna hear it!" Rocket shouted. "Get down here! I need those skinny fingers a' yours right now!"

"I am Groot," he said, slowly rising from his seat, shuffling his feet as he moved along the metal floor toward the hatch.

"I can hear you draggin' yer feet!" Rocket screamed. Then there was the sound of something hitting metal, and then Rocket let out a for-real scream.

"Rabbit!" Thor exclaimed as he leaped to his feet from the pilot's seat. "Are you all right?"

"I'm great!" Rocket fumed. "There's no space down here, wires are crossed, I keep gettin' shocked every two seconds, and I just slammed my head on the ceiling. Everything's peachy!"

By the time Rocket finished his rant, Groot had made it to the hatch. He knelt down, and peered inside.

There was Rocket, shaking his head vigorously. He was lying down on his back, facing up, staring at tangled vines of wires that crisscrossed the ceiling. He only had a little space in between him and the wires.

"Today!" Rocket yelled, and Groot huffed.

"I am Grooo—" he started to say, but then his mind flashed to the words he'd read in Rocket's journal entry.

We still have him, even if he's different. We're lucky to have him.

I'm lucky to have him. It's like having a second chance.

Groot swallowed the retort that had been halfway out of his mouth.

Rocket didn't say anything to him. "Look, just use those twigs a' yours to grab that red wire there." Then he pointed at a red wire that was clipped at the end, exposing a thin strip of metal.

"I am Groot?"

"Wood does not conduct electricity," Rocket said in a frustrated tone. "Quit bein' such a baby."

The words stung Groot a little, but he did his duty. He dropped down into the hatch and reached out with his long, twig-like fingers and grabbed hold of the red wire. It sparked suddenly, but true to Rocket's word, nothing happened to Groot.

Rocket turned back to the garden of wires before him, and started to clip a blue one with a pair of pliers.

"Now hand me the red one," Rocket said.

Groot did as he was asked.

A moment later, Rocket had connected the blue and red wires, and the sparking had stopped altogether.

"I am Groot?" the tree creature said.

"Yeah, I think that did it," Rocket said.

Rocket squirmed out from the compartment, past the wires, and toward the hatch. Groot made sure he was already out of the hatch by the time Rocket got there. He offered a hand to Rocket and pulled him out.

"Hey, why you bein' so helpful? You do somethin' wrong?" Rocket asked. He squinted at Groot.

"I am Groot!" Groot said, defensively. His response was probably a little over-the-top.

"Ease up," Rocket said. "You're just awful nice all of a sudden, is all. Makes me think you did somethin' you shouldn'ta done, and yer tryin' to cover up for it."

Groot's eyes went wide.

Did he know about the tablet? How could he know about the tablet?

Suddenly Rocket started to laugh. "The look on your face was priceless! I'm sorry, I'm just messin' with ya, Groot."

Rocket turned away from Groot, and walked back toward the cockpit and Thor.

Groot huffed again, then went back to his seat. His wooden fingers found the edge of the tablet beneath the med pack, and he slid it out silently.

"I am Groot," he said, then went back to reading.

CHAPTER 17

ENTRY 3X-AFVN.13.21

We were walkin' down the hill, away from the flamin' wreck that had been the hovercar.

"I can't believe they let us just take that thing," I said, and I was mad. "That thing had no business bein' out on the road. It coulda killed us!"

"Technically, they didn't give it to us," Dey pointed out. "You stole it."

"We stole it," I corrected. "You were my accomplice."

"Fine, we stole it," Dey said.

We walked along the metal road,

feeling the weird purple rain hit our faces, an' for a brief moment, the silence an' all of it felt almost peaceful, like everything in the world was all right.

"So where were we before the stupid hovercar decided to quit working?" I asked.

Dey thought about it, then said, "I'd just asked what Meer Kaal had told you about the weapons cache."

So I told Dey.

"Aphos Prime?" he said, and his voice sounded all weird and singsongy.

"Aphos Prime," I said right back.

"Are you sure he said *Aphos* Prime?"

"As sure as I'm standin' here listenin' to you ask me the same question repeatedly," I answered. It was a little smart-alecky, but I figured if anyone could take it, it was Dey.

"That can't be," Dey said, and he got this kind of faraway look in his eye.

"Whaddaya mean?"

"Aphos Prime . . . that planet doesn't even exist anymore," Dey said.

"Well, Meer Kaal was pretty certain that it does, and that's where the weapons are hidden," I said evenly.

"You're absolutely sure?" Dey said. "Do you think he could have been lying to you?"

I had to roll my eyes at that one. "Listen, Dey," I said, setting him straight. "I can tell when anyone is lying. Anyone. N-E-ONE. An' this guy was tellin' the God's honest."

"But how do you know?" Dey pressed.

"Because," I said, "I told him I worked for Thanos."

"You did what?"

"You heard me." I grinned.

"And what did he say?" Dey asked, genuinely interested.

"Well, it wasn't so much what he said, as what he did." Then I explained about the whole pants thing.

Dey laughed. "I don't believe it."

"Believe it. At least we're not the ones who have to clean that up."

We chuckled over that for a few, then Dey turned back to the whole Aphos Prime thing. "Aphos Prime was supposedly destroyed years ago," he said.

"Guess it's not as destroyed as you think."

We were almost at the bottom of the hill, having walked a long way. The rain was falling steady, and I could see the little town with the bar where Drax was doubtless still waiting for me.

I was just about to say good-bye to Rhomann Dey, when he turned to me and said, "I'm gonna need a little more of your help, Rocket."

I hate when people say that.

ENTRY 3X-AFVN.13.22

I was done goin' rogue on this one, an' I decided it was best if I brought in the rest of the troops. So we headed back to the bar to meet up with Drax and, when we got there, we contacted Quill, who was with Gamora an' Groot.

We sat at the table with Drax, listening to him tell us a really long story about his childhood. At least I think it was about his childhood. I was sort of half listening, half thinking we should just leave an' not get any further involved than I already was.

By the time the other three got there, Drax had finished his story, and was laughing like crazy, and slamming the table with his hand so hard it cracked the top. Dey and I exchanged glances, not sure where we had missed the joke.

"So what's the deal?" Quill said as he got to the table. "You guys were supposed to meet us back at the *Milano* an hour ago."

"Yeah, I see you were so concerned that you sent out a search party," I shot back.

Quill instantly got his hackles up. "Hey, I was just respecting your right to privacy."

As usual, Gamora was the voice of reason. "Will you two idiots shut up?" she said. "Rhomann Dey, Rocket said you need us."

"Yeah, what can the Guardians of the Galaxy do for the Nova Corps?" Quill said, and he sat down, leaned back in his chair, and put his hands behind his head. I think he was relishing the chance to have a little somethin' on Dey. Especially considering we had to ask the Nova Corps for a tow after the *Milano* was wrecked by that Van'Lan creature. Quill and I don' see eye-to-eye on much, but

I had to say I saw where he was comin' from here.

"First, I just want you to know that it is killing me to have to ask you for help, Star-Munch," Dey said.

Star-Munch? That was the funniest thing I ever heard. I swear, I'm gonna use that one from now on.

"It's Star-Lord," Quill said hotly.

"Yeah, I know," Dey said. "Anyway, I need you to hack into the Hall of Records back on Xandar."

Gamora peered at Dey, then she turned her head to look at me. "Rocket, what is going on here?" she asked.

"Don't look at me, this isn't my idea," I said.

"Rocket's right. He helped me get a, uh, piece of information that I needed," Dey started. "And now I need to confirm something by checking with the Hall of Records."

"Then why don't you just access the database yourself?" Gamora asked.

Dey didn't say anything, then Quill's eyes got real big an' bright.

"Unless you can't access the database yourself because it's forbidden," Quill said, suddenly very pleased with himself.

"I wouldn't say it's forbidden," Dey said carefully. "More like classified."

"C'mon, Quill, what's the harm? We just go back to the *Milano*, hack into the database, get the info Dey needs, an' we're on our way offa this dump," I said. It sounded like a good plan to me.

"Wait a second," Quill said. "We're not criminals anymore, right? And what happens to us if we get caught doing this? We'd be criminals again, right?"

"Your logic is astoundin'," I said.

"It is," Drax agreed, without a trace of sarcasm. "It's so crystal clear, the way he thinks."

"What if I told you the fate of the galaxy was at stake?" Dey said.

"When is it not?" Gamora said. Then she pulled on Quill's arm. "Come on, Peter. Let's get back to the ship and get this done."

"What?" Quill said. "Why, we're still—"

"No, we're not 'still,'" she said. "We're going to help Dey get the information he needs, and then we're going to leave."

"Give me one good reason why we should help him," Quill protested.

"Because Dey stuck his neck out for us when no one else did," Gamora said.

"And he's a decent guy," I added.

Oh, you shoulda seen the way they all looked at me after I said that.

"What?" I said. "Don't look at me funny. It's true!"

CHAPTER 18

ENTRY 3X-AFVN.13.45

The walk back to the hangar where the *Milano* was being repaired was dull and uneventful. Well, mostly dull. There was the usual bickering and arguing that we do, but I guess we're sort of a family, right? That's what families do. They fight. Maybe not as much as we do.

Still, family.

Anyway.

We planned out exactly what was supposed to happen. We were gonna log into a Xandarian gaming session, and use that as a back door for hacking into the Hall of Records. The *Milano*'s computer wasn't part of any network, so theoretically, there'd be no way for the Nova Corps to trace the transmission back to us.

Theoretically.

Actually? Now that I see this all typed out like this? It sounds like a buncha gibberish that even I don't believe.

By the time we got back to the *Milano*, the repairs to the ship were almost done. Sure, there were patches in some places, and the thing coulda used a new coat a' paint. But on the whole, it looked pretty good, all things considered.

"Rocket, you and Dey head inside," Gamora said. "Start the search. We'll look over everything out here and help finish up with the repairs."

With Drax, Gamora, Quill, and Groot outside, Dey and I went into the *Milano* and settled into the cockpit. I switched on the core computer system, and waited for it to boot up.

"Takes a minute or so," I said, pointing at the computer. "It's old."

"Just like you," Dey said.

Man, I liked this guy.

The computer whirred and clicked for a few seconds, until it was back online. Then I headed straight for the Xandarian gaming site like Dey said. Once we were in, I started the hack.

Dey an' I were sitting there waiting for the Hall of Records to pop up onscreen, when I felt somethin' in my back.

Somethin' made a' metal.

Then I heard three words that no one ever wants to hear.

"Hello, dead men."

CHAPTER 13

ENTRY 3X-AFVN.13.51

"Are you freaking kidding me?"

I didn't expect Dey to lose his cool like that. But he was pretty upset.

I guess I didn't blame him too much. After all, the only reason why Meer Kaal was standing there in the *Milano*, missing his prosthetic ear and holding a weapon to our backs, was because a' me.

"No kidding," Meer Kaal said. "This is deadly serious. Now keep your eyes facing the computer while I fry your insides."

"Wait a second," Dey said, all worked

up as his eyes bored into mine. "I just want to get this straight. Are you telling me that when you sneaked back out of the holding cell, you didn't bother to seal up the hole?"

"Yep," I answered.

"You had the presence of mind to steal his *ear*, but you couldn't seal up a freaking hole?" Dey continued.

"Yep," I repeated.

Dey turned around to face Meer Kaal. "Is this one-hundred-percent true?"

"One-hundred-percent," Meer Kaal said, and he raised the weapon until it was centered right between Rhomann Dey's eyes. "You know too much, Rhomann Dey. I'm going to destroy you and that horrible, rabid creature, and then my secret will be safe once more. Say good-bye."

He clicked the safety off his weapon. The guy clearly meant business.

"Wait!" I said.

"What now?" Meer Kaal replied, and he sounded pretty angry. Well, not angry. More like frustrated. Which I could see. I've been told before that I tend to try people's patience.

"How do we know you were even tellin' the truth?" I said to Meer Kaal. "Maybe you were lyin' to us the whole time. You are Kree, right? Aren't you able to resist all kinds of interrogation techniques?"

This seemed to confuse Meer Kaal. He just stood there for a while, like he was considering what I had just told him.

"Yes, of course I'm Kree, I . . ." Meer Kaal said, and then his voice slowly trailed off. I think in that instant he realized that I had tripped him up. That if he actually had been lyin' to us, he wouldn't have had to bother with coming back to kill us. The only reason to show up at the *Milano* is if he had been telling the truth the whole time.

I bet that *really* made him mad.

Judging by the way he shoved the weapon in Dey's face, I think it did.

"That's it," he snarled. "The time for talking has passed. Now is the time for dying!"

I shrugged my shoulders and looked forward. "Well, okay, if that's the way you want it. But I think you're makin' a big mistake."

"Oh, you do, do you?" Meer Kaal sneered. "Well, guess what, you furry freak? No one cares what you think!"

"I am Groot!"

Man, was I glad to see the little guy. I mean, it wasn't like the big Groot that I had been used to in the past. That guy was huge, an' would just come in an' save my butt all the time.

But there was little Groot, apparently about to do the exact same thing.

He jumped right on Meer Kaal's back, and started pounding away.

I was so prouda him! Givin' Meer Kaal a beatdown just like I woulda done, if I wasn't sittin' in a seat turned the other way with a weapon at my back!

Then the rest of the Guardians stormed in. Groot was on Meer Kaal and wouldn't let go until Drax punched Kaal in the gut and he crumpled onto the ground in a one-eared heap.

"Who is this?" Drax asked.

"It's that weirdo from the street," Gamora said, recognizing him.

"That," Dey said, "is Meer Kaal. The one who would still be in Nova custody, if it wasn't for a certain Rocket." He glared at me accusingly.

Geez. No good deed goes unpunished, am I right?

"That sounded very judgey," I said.

ENTRY 3X-AFVN.13.62

I wish I coulda taken a picture. Drax sat on top a' Meer Kaal to contain him while we got the job done. Actually *on top a'* him. It was unbelievable.

I went back to hacking the Hall of Records database. We got in an' looked around, until I was able to access the classified file on Aphos Prime. We transferred the info directly to Rhomann Dey, an' then we got out before anyone at the Hall of Records could have detected us.

And that was it.

"Looks like I owe the Guardians of the Galaxy a debt," Dey said as he walked down the ramp to the repair dock below, marching a bound-and-tied Meer Kaal in front of him, the rest of us trailing behind.

"Yeah, it looks like you do," I said.

Gamora shot me a look. "Rocket," she said admonishingly.

I always feel bad when she does that. No one can make me feel bad like she does. I guess you have to wonder what you did that was so bad that even the daughter of Thanos is angry at you.

Anyway.

"No, he's right," Dey said. "I do owe you one. Because of the help you gave, we'll be able to save more lives."

"I'll walk ya out," I said to Dey, waving off the others. We walked away from the *Milano*, and toward the big hangar doors that led back into town.

"This has been an experience," I said. And I meant it.

"Same here," Dey said. "If you'd told me after the first time I saw you that one day we'd be working together, I wouldn't have believed it."

"Me either," I said. I meant that, too.

"I wish upon you both a painful and

devastating death!" Meer Kaal vowed as he struggled against the restraints.

I grinned. "Yeah, well."

"See ya round the galaxy, Rocket," Dey said, patting me on the shoulder.

I shot him a quick wave, then turned around, and walked back to the *Milano*.

"I did ask you not to touch the controls, didn't I?"

"You did."

Groot looked up from the tablet. From his vantage point toward the back of the small ship, he could see Rocket sitting in the pilot's chair. Standing next to him, hands held up in protest, was Thor.

"Then WHY. ARE. YOU. TOUCHING. THEM?" Rocket yelled.

"Because you asked me to," Thor said, his voice surprisingly calm.

"Oh yeah? An' when did I say that?" Rocket fired back.

"I am Groot," said the tree creature.

"You stay outta this," Rocket threw over his shoulder. "I wasn't talkin' ta you!"

"The tree is correct," Thor said. "You asked me to sit at the controls while you were down the hatch, effecting repairs."

"Ah!" Rocket said, leaping up, standing on his seat. He still wasn't anywhere close to being eye-to-eye with the Asgardian, but he was a little closer. "SIT at the controls! Not TOUCH the controls! Do you see the difference? Can you grasp it?"

"I am sorry, Captain," Thor said, his tone placating. "I defer to you, of course."

"OH YEAH?" Rocket yelled, and it took him a second to realize that Thor had actually apologized, and reaffirmed that he was, in fact, in charge of the ship. Upon realizing that, he calmed down almost right away.

"Well, just don't touch the controls, is all I'm

sayin'," Rocket muttered, his voice subdued.

"Duly noted," Thor replied.

"I am Groot."

Thor sighed, and smiled at Groot. "Just what I was thinking."

CHAPTER 20

While Rocket fiddled with the controls at the pilot's station, Thor walked to the back of the ship, his right hand pressed against the hull as he leaned down to avoid smacking his head.

"I am Groot," the tree creature said, looking up from his seat.

"Most Asgardians are fairly tall, yes," Thor replied. "We get used to ducking. You have been quiet for most of the journey. Preparing yourself?"

"I am Groot." He shrugged.

"I understand," Thor said. "Sometimes the best thing you can do is take your mind off an impending task."

"I am Groot," he replied.

"Yes," Thor said. "I suppose it is an almost impossible task we have ahead of us."

All was quiet on the ship for a few moments as Rocket navigated, Thor and Groot both lost in their own thoughts.

"Hey, Thor!" Rocket called out, turning from his navigation panel to face Thor and Groot. "Tell me about these dwarves again."

"The dwarves of Nidavellir," Thor said. "The dwarves forge weapons for the Asgardians. In return, we offer protection."

"So it's like a protection racket?" Rocket asked.

"What's a protection racket?" Thor said.

"Exactly what you just described."

"When you say it like that, it seems like a bad thing," Thor observed.

"I didn't say it like that," Rocket said. "*You* said it like that."

"Oh look, asteroids!" Thor said, pointing toward the front window of the ship.

Immediately Rocket swiveled around in his chair. "What? Where?" he said, his voice filled with urgency. Realizing quickly that there were no asteroids, and it was just Thor bowing out of the conversation, Rocket let out a fake chuckle.

"Ha," he said out loud. "This is me laughing."

"It's a good sound," Thor said, before sitting back down.

Groot watched as Thor peered out the window into the vast sea of space, and Rocket focused once more on flying the ship. They would reach their destination soon.

Seeing that his two travel companions were sufficiently occupied, Groot turned his attention back to the tablet.

CHAPTER 21

ENTRY 3X-AFVN.313

I am not in my happy place right now. In fact, I'm so far away from my happy place, I couldn't even see it if you gave me a freakin' telescope.

An' it's all because a' this "rescue mission."

Ugh. Even the sound of it hurts my ears. "Rescue mission." It sounds like somethin' ya do that you don't get paid for.

"That's exactly what it is."

That's what Gamora said to me when I told her what I thought of when I heard the words "rescue mission."

"Okay, it's like, I get the idea of a rescue mission," I said, layin' out my case. "People need our help. Cool. I'm fine with that. But what I don't get is why shouldn't they pay us after we help them out?"

"Because we're heroes," Quill chimed in. "We're the Guardians of the Galaxy. We should be guardian . . . ing."

"I am Groot."

Ha! Groot was right. "Yeah, that's not a word," I agreed.

"It is now," Quill said, an' he shot me daggers with his eyes, an' turned back to the ship's controls. I made a disgusted noise from the back of my throat. Quill was just playin' the part of selfless savior so Gamora would like him. Suck-up.

"Rocket."

Gamora talkin'. Always the voice of reason. Sometimes I really hated reason. But I liked Gamora. Talk about contradictions.

"We have to help them. We're the only ship in the quadrant fast enough to reach them. If we don't help them, people will die," Gamora said.

There she goes, tuggin' at the heartstrings.

"I hate when you say things like that," I grumbled.

"When she says things like what?" Drax asked.

"That if we don't help, people will die!"

"It's true!" Gamora shouted.

"I know it's true!" I yelled right back. "I just don't like it!"

So I sat there in my seat, lookin' out the cockpit, and fumed for a few seconds. I knew Gamora was right. An' I knew that goin' ta help those people was right, too. But sometimes, old habits are hard to shake, ya know?

"Awright, fine, we'll do it your way," I said at last, gracious and compromising as always. "We'll go save the day, again."

"Thank you," Gamora said, but I suspect she didn't really mean it.

"You're welcome," I said, certain that I didn't mean it. "But I have one request. One humble, lowly, little request."

"Shoot," Quill said, flippin' a couple a' switches on a side panel.

"When we are done, and everyone is safe and happy, if they offer to pay us for our services, CAN WE AT LEAST FREAKIN' ACCEPT?"

"I am Groot."

"Exactly," I said, jammin' my thumb toward the little guy to emphasize my point. "Groot gets it!"

"Fine," Gamora said. "If they offer, you can accept."

It seemed like she was cavin', but I know Gamora better than that. More like she knew what it was gonna take to shut me up, so she just said what I wanted to hear.

She's good.

"Awright, now that we have that settled, what ridiculous situation are we getting ourselves into this time?" I said, because I knew that the situation would be 100 percent ridiculous, otherwise we wouldn't be getting involved.

"Well," Quill said, looking at the screen in front of him. "It's not . . . great."

"Not great," I said. "What does 'not great' mean, exactly?"

"Not great," Drax answered. "It is obvious. It means—"

"I know what 'not great' means," I said, cutting Drax off. "I mean, what are the SPE-CI-FICS of this rescue mission?"

Quill laughed. "Oh, those? Yeah, you're not gonna like it."

ENTRY 3X-AFVN.334

Oh man, Quill was not wrong.

This rescue mission was gonna stink on ice.

It turned out the ship that needed rescuing was a mining vessel of "unknown origin." That means they didn't say where they were from when they set off their distress beacon. So right off the bat, we had no way of knowin' if they were friendly, hostile, or anywhere in between. If they were Kree, or Xandarian, Skrull, or from the freakin' Planet Jerk.

Then it got better.

Did I say better? I meant worse.

The mining ship was stranded in the middle of an asteroid field. Apparently they got clipped by one of the asteroids, and it knocked out the ship's main engine and control thrusters. Without those, they had no way of getting out of the asteroid field. They confirmed it in their transmission that their ship had shields. But every time an asteroid hit, the shield integrity dropped.

When enough asteroids hit, the shield would go down for good, and bye-bye mining ship.

This meant that we were on a clock. We only had so long to get to the ship and pull 'em outta the asteroid field before it just didn't matter anymore.

"Does anyone else think this rescue mission blows?" I asked. "Raise yer hand."

I raised mine.

Groot looked at me an' raised his hand, too.

Good kid.

"Don't raise your hand," Quill said to us. "Anybody with your hand up, put it down. That's gross!"

"How is that gross?" I asked. "I'm just bein' honest!"

"Well, your honesty is gross!"

"Grow up," Gamora said to all of us.

CHAPTER 22

ENTRY 3X-AFVN.37

Man, did I miss the *Milano*. I wish I'd been able to finish the repairs to it. When we crashed on Berhert, the ship had been in pretty bad shape. Meaning it was in pieces. Like, one piece over there, another over there, hey, look in that tree! It's the cockpit!

I worked on that thing like crazy, puttin' my heart an' soul an' sweat an' spit into it. But I never got to complete the fixes, 'cause Yondu and the Ravagers showed up, and started a whole tussle with me an' Groot an' Nebula.

Well, not Nebula so much, 'cause she

rolled over on us pretty quick. Tricky minx. She's good.

We got captured by the Ravagers, who were technically doing a job for these people called the Sovereign, on account of I sorta stole some anulax batteries from them. That's a whole other story, but it's a good one. Anyway, the Ravagers were tryin' to capture the Guardians, Quill especially, an' bring 'em back to the Sovereign, so they could collect a ton of units.

They managed to get me an' Groot. They took us off planet to their ship, the *Eclector*, so it was bye-bye *Milano*. From there, we busted out, went to fight Ego, save Quill, save the universe, blah blah blah.

I never saw the *Milano* again.

So now we got this new ship, which is fast, but not as fast as I would like. It's just not made to handle the kinda speed we like to squeeze outta the engines. Not like the *Milano*—now, *that* ship was built for speed. You could fly that thing and push the envelope and then some, and it held together beautifully. This one? You so much as *think* about exceeding pressure limits an' speed thresholds an' technical stuff like that, an' the whole ship starts to shake. What a baby.

You could feel the vibrations comin' through the seats, that's how bad it was.

You know how else you could tell it was bad? Gamora leaned over to me, an' said, "Is it supposed to do this?"

Meaning the ship.

I said, "No. But it's doing it anyway."

I thought that was a pretty evenhanded response, all things considering.

Then I checked on our ETA to the mining ship. We had actually made decent time, even with this bucket a' bolts threatening to fall apart at any second. I figured we had about another twenty minutes or so, an' we'd be there. The asteroid field wasn't on visual yet, but we had it on our navigation system, an' we were already plotting a course through it to reach the ship.

By "plotting a course," I mean that I looked at the screen, saw lots of little individual asteroids, an' realized I would just have to wing it. Of course, I didn't say this to anyone else. Not yet, anyway.

"When we get there, we're gonna have to be quick," Quill said. "We can't afford any screwups."

"Who are you talkin' to, exactly?" I shot right back. I don't know, it felt like he was attackin' me or somethin'.

"He's talking to all of us, Rocket," Gamora said.

"And, I'm talking to Rocket specifically," Quill had to add.

See, I knew it.

"If you got somethin' ta say, Quill, just say it." I wasn't in the mood for his little games.

"I'm just saying, we don't want anything to go wrong with the rescue. We're on a tight timeline, and we're only gonna have a few minutes to transfer the crew from that ship to ours before the asteroids destroy it."

"Huh," I said, deciding whether to bite my tongue or not. I think I mighta actually bitten my tongue, now that I think about it. It didn't help. "'Cause it sounded to me like you were singling me out."

"He wasn't," Gamora said.

"I was," Quill said.

"I hate everyone on this ship!" I yelled, an' then I turned back to my console.

"Why do you hate me?" Drax said. "I've done nothing. It's unwarranted."

"Fine, I don't hate you," I said.

"I am Groot."

"Or you, either."

"Great, so it's just me and Gamora," Quill said.

"I don't hate Gamora!"

"So it's just me?"

"Just you!"

Quill looked at me an' wrinkled up his eyebrows that way he does when he thinks he's right, an' said, "Then just say that next time! You make everybody else feel bad when you say stuff like that."

"Will you two morons please stop arguing so we can plan the rescue?" Gamora said. The look on her face was pretty serious. I'd seen that look a lot of times, except usually she had a sword in her hands an' she was about to separate some poor guy's head from his shoulders.

So I shut up.

ENTRY 3X-AFVN.389

"Coming up on the asteroid field . . . now," Quill said.

At that point, we got our first look at

the asteroid field on full visual. It was a monster. I'd never see one like it before. It wasn't that the asteroids were so big, or anything like that. It was that there were so *many*. An' they weren't just floating there in space, either. Like, usually when we encounter an asteroid field, they're just kinda rollin' there, mindin' their own business. An' because we're travelin' at crazy speeds, they go by fast. But because they're movin' at a relatively slower speed, it's easier for us to avoid 'em.

That wasn't the case with this asteroid field. Those rocks were *moving*. An' they were packed so tight, it was like they were forming a solid wall. I slumped back in my seat, an' for a second, I really was wonderin' just what we were gonna do.

"That does not look good," Gamora said at last. I was glad she spoke first, 'cause if Quill had, I probably woulda thumped him.

"I am Groot."

"Yeah, I have to agree with ya, pal." I nodded. "It's gonna take some real fancy flyin' to get us past that mess."

"Good thing you've got me," Quill said.

"No!" Gamora said, and she stormed right over to where Quill was sitting, grabbed his hands, and took them off the controls. "I'm not going through this again, not after last time."

By "last time," Gamora meant the incident directly after I stole the anu-lax batteries from the Sovereign. We were makin' our getaway, with an entire fleet of Sovereign omnicrafts in pursuit. There might have been some sort of conversation between me an' Quill about who was the better pilot, an' it's possible that, on some level, we mighta been at least a little responsible for the ship's eventual destruction when we flew it through . . .

. . . an asteroid field.

Ugh. I hate it when people who aren't me are right.

"Let Rocket fly us through," Gamora said with authority. "Rocket, can you do it?"

I looked at the screen in front of me, and then at the actual asteroid field through the cockpit window.

"Can I get us through the asteroid field and reach the ship before it's toast?" I said.

(I paused for dramatic effect. It was very dramatic, and very effective.)

"Yeah."

Now all I had to do was deliver.

CHAPTER 23

ENTRY 3X-AFVN.391

Have you ever tried to fly a ship through an asteroid field when you've got every single person on board your craft tellin' you exactly what you're doin' wrong, an' how you could do it better?

'Cause I have.

"What part of 'left' don't you get?!"

"Up there! Right there! In front of your face!"

"I am Groot!"

"How can you fail to notice the asteroids?"

"I am Groot!"

"Right! Not left. Right!"

That's about all I was hearin' for a solid minute before I'd had it.

"SHUT UP! ALLA YOU!" I shouted at the top of my lungs. "I'm flyin' this crate, an' if you don't like the way I'm doin' it, keep it to yourself! Now, if you'll excuse me, I have an asteroid field to navigate!"

This was the worst bit of flying I'd ever had to do. The asteroids were traveling so fast, and packed in so tight, I wasn't even sure if this new ship would be able to squeeze through the cracks.

So far, I'd been lucky. Sure, we'd gotten dinged a few times by a stray asteroid here and there . . . and here . . . and there . . . but on the whole, we were doin' okay.

"Will someone turn that blasted alarm off!" The ship's proximity alert was there to warn us of any incoming objects. But since we entered the asteroid field, all we had was incoming objects. The alarm wouldn't stop blaring, an' it was hurting my sensitive ears.

I don't want to brag too much, but the flying was pretty fancy. I was avoiding cluster after cluster of speeding space rock, an' makin' it look easy. Sort of.

But there's always a danger in a pilot gettin' cocky or overconfident in his own abilities. Not that that's what happened to me. I'm a grounded sort of guy. Just sayin'.

I guess I'm sayin' that, because that's right when a small asteroid clipped our right wing, and sent us into a spiral.

WHAM! (That was the asteroid.)

WHOA! (That was us, as we started to spiral out of control.)

Suddenly we were goin' around an' around at a crazy speed. I felt my stomach hit my throat, go back down, then come up again, an' it kept on doin' it. I'm sure everyone else wanted to hurl, too. I yanked hard on the ship's yoke, trying to stop the roll, but I couldn't. Laws of physics were in control now, an' they're very hard laws to break.

I couldn't stop the roll, but I still had some control over the ship's lateral movement. So I was able to avoid the asteroids as we rolled through the field. It was less than ideal, but it was the only thing I could do.

"We need to stabilize this, or we're dead!" Gamora yelled.

"Yeah, I know that!" I said. I mean, I did know that. It wasn't like I didn't understand our situation.

Quill ran a quick diagnostic to figure out why we couldn't stop the roll. The results came back fast, an' they weren't great. "The asteroid took out the directional thrusters on the right wing," Quill shouted. "There's no way to counterthrust to stop the roll!"

That sucked, but it was true. In order to stop the roll, we'd need the counter-thrust from both wings to right the ship. With only the thrusters on the left wing operational, firin' 'em would only speed up the roll.

As I was fightin' the controls, tryin' not to get us all killed, I heard this little voice behind me.

"I am Groot."

"What?" I said, an' I felt like my eyes were gonna pop outta my head. "No, you're not! No way! Sit down an' stay down!"

"You're not going out there, Groot!" Gamora yelled.

"No," Drax said. "Because I'm going out there."

"WHAT?!?"

(Everybody said that at the same time. You shoulda been there, it was actually kinda funny.)

CHAPTER 24

ENTRY 3X-AFVN.392

I couldn't believe it. I mean, I could believe it, but I couldn't believe it, if you get me. Drax was ALWAYS the one who "went out there" during a hazardous space flight to fix somethin', or to shoot at somethin'. This situation was ideal, I guess, because it provided him with an opportunity to fix AND shoot, in some cases at the same time.

In that context, it made perfect sense.

"You're not goin' out there!" I yelled.

"I'm the only one who can fix the ship," Drax said. He was already grabbin' a holographic spacesuit from the storage bin, an' he had a rifle clutched in his left hand.

"I said, you're not goin' out there, because I figured a way out of our problem!"

"You did?" Quill said.

"You sound surprised," I said menacingly. "I don't think I like that."

"Forget him," Gamora said. "What is it?"

"I'm gonna cut the engines, then hit full reverse thrust," I said.

It's funny. Once the words came out of my mouth, the idea sounded less great than when it was just in my head.

"That is not gonna work," Quill said immediately.

"How do you know?" Gamora asked.

"Yeah, how would you know?" I chimed in.

"I am Groot."

"Well, he's always gonna take your side," Quill grumbled.

"Look, just trust me on this. We need to cut our forward momentum to kill the roll. I think this will do it."

I hoped it would do it.

"What about the asteroids?" Drax asked.

"Take a seat, an' start shooting," I said.

That was a request that made Drax very happy. He put the rifle and the spacesuit back, climbed into the seat, strapped in, and started to blast away.

"Everybody hang on!" I yelled. Then I cut the engines completely. We were still rolling, our momentum carryin' us along. But at least we weren't adding to the problem. Then, I hit the retro-thrusters full on. Everyone woulda been thrown clear a' their seats if we hadn't all been strapped in.

The roll was starting to slow, just a little, but the ship didn't like what I was doin' to it. It groaned, and yawed a little, an' I saw some sparks comin' from the forward flight bay. That was probably not a good sign.

"I don't think she can take much more of this!" Quill yelled over the sound of the engines.

"Don't think we have any choice!" Gamora said.

A hundred and ten percent correct.

The ship was still rolling, but not as fast. We were slowin' down with every revolution. There was this loud cracking sound, and we all kind of looked around, concerned, because that's not a sound you ever want to hear on a spaceship. It sounded like someone tore off a chunk of a wing.

"Look," said Drax, his voice flat. "There goes a chunk of the wing."

Sure enough, we'd lost the tip of the right wing. It wasn't a big loss, considering the directional thrusters had already flamed out. I could still fly the ship without it.

The roll continued to slow, until finally I killed the retro-thrusters. Then I gunned the main engine, and shoved the yoke forward as hard I could. Drax was blasting away at an asteroid heading straight for the cockpit.

It was gonna be a close one.

ENTRY 3X-AFVN.41

"They don't all have to be that close," Quill muttered, bright and sunny as always. He was probably just bitter that he hadn't thoughta that brilliant save.

As for me? I couldn't believe we made it! At the last second, Drax nailed the asteroid with a perfect shot an' split the thing right in the middle. I regained forward control of the ship, an' we breezed right between the asteroid halves, without so much as a scratch.

"Aw, c'mon!" I hollered. "If they're not that close, then where's the drama? The majesty?"

"Do you have any idea how much it's gonna cost to repair this ship?" Quill said.

"No, not really," I fired back. "I'm not an accountant."

We were outta immediate danger, but we were still surrounded by a fair amount of just-about-to-happen danger. The asteroid field was a nightmare, and our ship wasn't in the best shape.

"Where is that mining ship?" I called out to Gamora, who was peering intently at her scanner.

"According to this, we're practically on top of it. We should have visual any second now," she said. Then her brow furrowed as she leaned closer to the screen. "That's . . . that can't be right."

"Whoa, whoa, what can't be right?" Quill said. He sounded worried.

I was worried, too. Anytime someone like Gamora says, *that can't be right*, you better believe it's not right. She doesn't kid around, not about stuff like that.

"The mining ship—there's a massive radiation surge coming from within," Gamora said. "I've never seen anything like it."

"It didn't register before?" Drax asked.

Gamora shook her head. "Nothing until just now. It's still there . . . it's like a pulse. There's an ebb and a flow to the wave. Like it's expanding and contracting."

"Maybe it's something they mined?" I asked, tryin' ta figure it out. "Some kinda ore?"

"Could be," Gamora said. "Either way,

make sure we engage the radiation safety mode on the holographic spacesuits."

"Yeah," I added. "The last thing we need is to not get a reward AND get radiation poisoning."

CHAPTER 25

ENTRY 3X-AFVN.49

"Any response?" Quill asked.

Gamora had been trying to hail the mining vessel since we'd first detected the radiation surge coming from their ship.

"Nothing," Gamora said. "Maybe their communications relay is down."

"They coulda lost it when they became disabled in the asteroid field," I said. It made sense. At least it was plausible. But I still didn't like it. Somethin' about this whole thing just wasn't sittin' right with me.

"There she is," Quill said, an' everyone looked forward. Just up ahead, caught in a pocket of asteroids, we could make out the silhouette of the mining vessel. It wasn't too big, maybe fifteen, twenty meters long. It was dark, no lights visible anywhere.

"This is creepy," I said.

"I agree with Rocket," Drax said, staring at the derelict vessel. "It's creepy in a way that I find deeply uncomfortable. I'll describe it further to you."

"No, I'm good," I said.

"Yeah, we're all good, Drax," Quill interjected. "We're all creeped out right now."

"I am Groot."

"Yeah, I can understand wanting to cut an' run right now," I said to Groot. He wasn't wrong. For a sapling, he had really learned a lot. An' he was kinda smart. Must take after me.

"We can't just leave them here,"

Gamora said. "Pull alongside. We'll use spacesuits to enter the craft and look for survivors. Then we'll get the hell out of here."

I looked at Gamora. "Who am I to say no?" I said, an' I brought the ship in closer.

The ship looked abandoned. As we moved in, we could make out window portals in the hull, but we didn't see any signs of life in 'em. If the crew was still alive, they must be hidden somewhere?

Then it hit me.

"The radiation surge," I said, out loud, apparently, because everyone turned around to look at me. "Whatever's causin' it, the crew must be hidin' from it. Maybe they've got a radiation-proof chamber?"

"That explains why we can't see any-body," Gamora said.

"Yeah," Quill added. "That, or they're already dead."

"Always lookin' on the bright side," I said. Usually, it was my job to be as pessimistic as Quill. More so, even. An' yet, here I was, gettin' in close to a creepy-lookin' spaceship with no visible crew, the thing crawlin' with radiation, an' I was gonna go inside lookin' for survivors.

What was wrong with me?

ENTRY 3X-AFVN.53

"There, grab on to that rung!"

I almost missed it. If Quill hadn't pointed it out to me, I would have over-shot the ship completely. I grabbed out, an' my hand barely touched the metal rung. Pulling myself over, I slapped my other hand onto the next rung.

"You all right?" Quill asked.

"Yeah, yeah," I said. I probably shoulda said thank you, but I have a hard time with stuff like that. Besides, he knew I meant it.

I looked over my shoulder, an' there was Drax wearing his holographic space-suit. He was on the other side of the ship's hull. Quill was just up ahead, using the metal rungs that lined the outside of the ship's hull to pull himself up to the cockpit.

"You see anythin' inside, any sign a' life?" I said over the comm-link. I knew the answer to the question even before I asked it.

Quill shook his head. "Nothing. I can't see anything inside. Not even a light flashing on any computer," he said. "Gamora, what's the radiation reading?"

Gamora an' Groot were back on the ship. In case somethin' went wrong, they'd be there to bail us out. Or leave us, because we were already dead.

"Reading is steady," she said, loud and

clear over the comm-link. "Still coming and going."

"Awright," I said, anxious to have this whole thing behind us. "Let's open the hatch an' get on with it. I don't wanna be here all day."

"That would be impossible," Drax said. "We spent most of the day getting here."

"Let's depressurize the ship's cabin so we can open the hatch," Quill said.

I moved along the metal rungs and over to the hatch. There was a keypad next to it, where you could enter the code that would cause the ship's main cabin to lose pressure, so its atmosphere would equal the atmosphere out in space. Then the hatch could be opened, an' we could get inside.

There was just one problem.

"Hey, Quill," I said. "The cabin's already depressurized."

What the hell was goin' on here?

ENTRY 3X-AFVN.55

Total darkness. That's all we saw inside the ship. The only light was comin' from our spacesuits. But all the computers, all the ship's systems, everythin' was dead.

Me, Drax, and Quill were inside. I walked over to the control panel next to the interior hatch so I could re-pressurize the cabin. At least that way, if there were any survivors, they wouldn't asphyxiate or die or nothin' when we brought 'em into the main cabin.

"There's nothing up here at all," Drax said, sounding kinda mystified.

"Look for the storage compartments," Quill said. "It's a mining ship, they gotta have 'em."

We headed toward the back of the ship, an' saw a tube with a ladder inside. The ladder went down.

"Who goes first?" I said. "I think Quill should, because he's the captain of this mission."

"Oh, so *now* I'm the captain of this mission?"

"SHUT. UP."

That was Gamora, her voice floating through from outside.

"I'll go," Drax said, "while you two cowards decide who is captain."

Drax brushed right past me, pushed his big honkin' shoulders into the tube, and climbed down.

"I am not a coward," Quill whispered to me.

"I never said you were," I shot back.

"Quill, Rocket."

Drax.

"Get down here. Now."

CHAPTER 26

ENTRY 3X-AFVN.57

I ducked into the tube first and climbed down. Quill was right behind me. When I hit the deck, an' I saw Drax, I knew we were in trouble.

Drax was lyin' facedown on the metal floor, an' he had a big foot on his head. The foot was connected to a leg, or what I guess was a leg. I couldn't tell.

The thing that had Drax pinned down looked kinda like a biped, y'know, two arms, two legs, a head, et cetera. Except it looked nothin' like one. It was all kinda lumpy, distorted . . . like someone took a lump a' dough, and stretched it all out to make somethin' that kinda looked like a person but wasn't.

"What the hell are you?" I said, right as Quill stepped down from the ladder.

Whatever the thing was, it was lookin' right at me. Its eyes were glowing a weird red color, an' they were pulsing, bright then dim, bright then dim. Then I saw somethin' behind the thing that made me look twice.

There was a small hole punched into the side a' the lower hull, somethin' we didn't notice when we did our first pass of the ship. It looked like something had torn right through the hull. An asteroid? Somethin' else?

Sitting right opposite the hole, embedded in the metal floor, was a small, glowing, red rock. The rock was throbbing, almost like it was alive, growing bright, then dim, bright then dim.

"Look, we don't want any trouble,"

Quill said, his hands held up in a classic we-mean-no-harm kinda way.

"Speak for yourself," I said. "I wouldn't mind a little trouble right about now. So how's about you take your foot off my friend's head, an' in return, I don't explode your body?"

The thing that had its foot pressed against Drax's head let out a weird hissing sound, like steam escaping. Then it started to groan this unholy moan, like it was in pain or somethin'.

"Rocket," Drax gritted out, sounding like he was in serious pain. "This thing's foot . . . it's burning through my spacesuit."

"What?" I said. "How is that even possible?"

The thing moaned even louder now, and pressed its foot into Drax's head. I couldn't figure out how a thing like that coulda gotten the drop on Drax. I mean, this is Drax we're talkin' about. Only the best warrior in the galaxy. (Do not tell him I said that.)

"If you could just take your foot off our friend's head, we'll clear outta here," Quill said, trying to sound authoritative and failing miserably as usual. "We came here looking for survivors. We don't want to hurt anybody."

The thing moaned again, an' this time, we heard somethin' movin' behind it.

"What was that?" I said. I don't mind tellin' you I was a little on edge at this point.

Then we heard this shuffling sound, and a low moan coming from the rear of the hold. I shined the light from my spacesuit toward the back an' saw 'em.

Three more a' these . . . things, distorted, misshapen, moaning, slowly shuffling toward us.

That was it. I was done playin' around. I pulled a weapon I had clipped to the back of my spacesuit, and got ready to open fire.

"Wait," Drax said, his face all scrunched up. "Don't shoot, Rocket."

"Is my hearing going?" I said. "It sounded a lot like you said, 'Don't shoot, Rocket,' which I know can't be possible."

"They don't mean us harm," Drax persisted, breathing heavily.

"Really? 'Cause that thing's foot is tryin' ta burn a hole through your head. That looks a lot like harm to me," I said.

"No, Rocket, he's right," Quill said, an' he put his hand on my weapon, pushing it down.

Normally that woulda set me off, an' I woulda lost my junk. But before I could react, Drax spoke up.

"I think these *are* the survivors," he said.

ENTRY 3X-AFVN.62

These poor jerks.

I didn't know what to do.

Drax didn't know.

Quill didn't know.

I don't think Gamora or Groot woulda known what to do, either.

When the mining ship got stuck in the asteroid field an' they lost their engines, they musta sent out the distress call. An' if everything had gone according to plan, we woulda come along, picked 'em up, an' that woulda been that.

Except it didn't go according to plan.

From what I could figure, that little red meteorite or whatever it was musta punched a hole right through the hull. Before the crew even knew what hit 'em, they were overcome by the radiation that the meteorite was giving off.

In the time it took us to get here, their bodies musta been ravaged by the radiation, changed, mutated . . . until they became the things we were lookin' at.

"We gotta get these guys offa this thing," I said. I don't know why I said it, or where it came from, but there it was.

"Rocket, I don't know if that's such a good idea," Quill said nervously.

"I don't care if it's the worst idea in the galaxy!" I shouted at Quill. "We're not just gonna leave these jerks here to die. They deserve better than that!"

"Rocket," Drax said, an' the way he said it was kinda gentle, so it caught me off guard.

"What, you're gonna fight me on this, too, Drax?"

The thing that had its foot on top a' Drax's head quivered for a moment, then crumpled to a heap on the floor. The others followed suit, one after the other. All four things had slumped to the metal floor, and were starting to glow on and off, bright then dim, bright then dim. And not just their eyes, either. This time it was their bodies. Their whole bodies.

"Rocket, I think they're dying," Drax said, sadly. "There is nothing we can do for them."

"Peter," Gamora radioed in. "You have to get off that ship now. The radiation levels are spiking through the roof!"

I looked over at the poor, miserable things on the ground, pulsing, glowing, an' I thought that Gamora was right.

There was nothing we could do for them. That made me sick. I wanted ta help. But if we stayed, somethin' bad was gonna happen to us, too.

It was a terrible call, the kinda call a captain never wants to have ta make.

The words caught in my throat. But

if there's one thing I know about bein' a captain, it's sometimes ya gotta make the tough decisions.

"Abandon ship," I said.

CHAPTER 27

ENTRY 3X-AFVN.653

Everything that happened after that was a blur. The things were just lyin' there, glowin' red, throbbing in time to the red meteorite. I didn't know exactly what it was, but I decided right then an' there that it was somethin' evil.

Me, Quill, an' Drax climbed back up the ladder, an' made our way to the hatch. We depressurized the cabin, opened the hatch, an' made our way out.

It took a minute or so for us to cross the distance between the derelict an' our ship. We made it to the hatch and climbed inside. As soon I entered, I heard Gamora yell, "Are you all in?!"

"We're in!" I screamed up to the flight deck.

Gamora wasn't wasting any time. As soon as she knew we were safely aboard, she hit the engines.

Next thing I knew, I was tumbling end over end, rolling toward the back of the hatch compartment, with Drax on top a' me, an' Quill on top a' him.

Normally, I woulda had some kinda snappy comeback or insult to say. But for the first time in a long time, I couldn't think of anything. Quill musta been feeling it, too, because we were both kinda just silent.

The engines were whining, an' I could feel the ship starting to shake itself apart again. I wasn't sure if the thing could handle the strain this time.

We climbed up to the flight deck an'

took our seats. Gamora was whizzing past the asteroids, dodging left an' right, at the same time she was keepin' an eye on the radiation scanner.

"It's building up to critical mass," Gamora said. "We need to be fifteen clicks from here in the next ten seconds or we're dead!"

"We need more speed," Quill said. He was right. As fast as this ship was, it was no *Milano*. I was pretty sure the *Milano* coulda covered that distance in time. I wasn't so sure about this one.

Gamora already had the ship runnin' at full tilt. I looked at the monitor next to me.

Eleven clicks to go.

Eight seconds left.

We weren't gonna make it.

We were gonna morph into red creepy-crawlies, just like those poor jerks back on the mining ship.

"Hang on!" Gamora screamed, an'

she did somethin' that I shoulda thought of, but I didn't. She hit the left directional, swinging us around backward. Then she killed the engine, an' hit the retro-thrusters full on.

The retros were the fastest engines the ship had, which made sense—they had to bring us to a dead stop as fast as possible. But turn 'em around in the other direction? Suddenly we MOVED.

"Three seconds!" I yelled.

Two clicks.

It was gonna

be

close.

ENTRY 3X-AFVN.655

Everything was white. That's all I could see. I was pretty sure I was dead.

Then the white started to fade, until everything went black. I could see outlines of things, but I didn't know where I was or what they were.

After a minute, I remembered everything that had been happening. The derelict, the red meteorite, the terrible thing that happened to the ship's crew. Us making it back, Gamora hightailing it outta there, an' then the explosion.

That's right, the explosion. The red meteorite had built up to critical mass, an' exploded. We made it out of the prime blast zone, but the shock wave had knocked the ship clear into another sector.

I blinked, or at least I think I was blinkin'. It took a while, but everythin' started to come into focus. I was in the cockpit, an' I saw the other Guardians there.

They were okay.

At least they looked okay.

Nobody was all mutated with glowin' red eyes.

The controls were so hot, they were

steaming. You couldn't even touch 'em without burnin' yer hand.

"Everybody who's not alive speak up," I said.

Gamora laughed.

"I am Groot."

Now I laughed. "I said speak up if you're *not* alive."

"I am Groot."

"See? Now he gets it," I said. I swiveled in my seat, and turned to face Gamora, who looked a little shook up but none the worse for wear. "That was some . . . halfway decent flying."

"I'll take that as a compliment," Gamora said.

"He's sulking because he knows you fly better than he does," Drax commented unhelpfully from his seat.

"That is not true," I shot back.

"Which part?" Quill asked. "The part about you sulking, or the part about Gamora being a better pilot?"

I had a sharp comment ready to cut Quill off at the knees, but then I thought about the crew we left behind on that derelict, and how we couldn't do anything to help 'em. Those red eyes.

Then, I just turned around in my seat, an' looked out the window.

ENTRY 3X-AFVN.657

"I am Groot?"

No one had said a word for a while, so when Groot popped up behind me, I was a little surprised. Everyone else was busy makin' repairs 'cause of all the damage we sustained during the aborted rescue.

"Yeah, squirt, what is it?"

He gave me a searching look. "I am Groot."

"Well . . . yeah. Look, don't go tellin' nobody, but yeah, I'm a little . . . sad, I guess?"

"I am Groot?"

"'Cause it's a really sad thing that happened. People dyin' like that . . . it shouldn't happen," I said.

"I am . . . Groot."

"Yep, but it does. Sooner or later."

"I am Groot?"

"Yeah, even to me."

"I . . . I . . ."

He didn't finish the sentence, just rested one of his little limbs on my arm and looked up at me, his eyes all big.

An' I didn't know what else to say.

CHAPTER 28

"What's this?" Thor said, staring at the object in his hand.

"What's it look like?" Rocket replied. "Some jerk lost a bet with me on Contraxia."

Thor considered the object in his hand. "He gave you his eye?" Thor said, as if trying to wrap his head around what exactly his diminutive companion had been doing with an artificial eyeball for years.

"No, he gave me a hundred credits," Rocket said. "I snuck into his room later that night and stole his eye."

In that moment, Groot realized that the eye Rocket had "obtained" from Skoort wasn't the same as the eye his friend had just handed to

Thor. But it did make him wonder—what was Rocket doing with all these artificial eyes and limbs in the first place?

Groot wasn't sure what to make of that. If nothing else, it was just a weird quirk—really, really weird. But it didn't really matter. After reading the journal entries, Groot had seen a different side of Rocket. Somewhere, buried deep within all that fur and sarcasm, there was a heart as big and as good as any Groot had ever seen. And it was on display now, right in front of him.

"Thank you, sweet rabbit," Thor said. Without any further ado, he removed the patch from his right eye and placed the artificial one into the socket. It made a wet sucking sound, and Groot was fascinated. He couldn't stop watching.

"Oooh, I woulda washed that," Rocket said. "The only way I could sneak it off Contraxia was up my—"

Rocket's thought was cut off midsentence by an alert from the pod's console.

"Hey, we're here!" Rocket said.

Groot leaned forward, trying to get a better view out of the cockpit. Darkness surrounded them. Wherever "here" was, it certainly didn't look inviting.

The next thing he knew, Groot saw Thor smacking the right side of his head with his hand. The artificial eye rolled around a little, like it was trying to adjust to its new surroundings.

"I don't think this thing works," Thor said, trying to focus. "Everything seems dark."

Once again, Groot looked outside the cockpit. They were supposed to be arriving at Nidavellir. They were supposed to be making a weapon that could destroy Thanos forever. But all he could see outside was a massive object floating in space, black and lifeless.

"It ain't the eye," Rocket said. Groot noticed the grim tone in his friend's voice.

EPILOGUE: WAKANDA

Rocket had fought harder than he had ever remembered fighting in his entire existence.

They all had. Every single one of them.

He had stood shoulder-to-shoulder with heroes from another world, people he had never met before. Together, they gave everything they had, all in one last, desperate attempt to stop Thanos.

Their goal was to prevent the Titan from obtaining the sixth and final Infinity Stone from a being called Vision.

They had failed.

And with a simple snap of his fingers, Thanos willed half of all living creatures in the universe away.

Before his eyes, Rocket saw people who had been fighting for their lives only moments before slowly dissolve, their bodies turning to dust, dissipating in the air, blowing away.

"I am Groot."

Rocket turned, and saw his friend and fellow Guardian slumped against a fallen tree. Rocket's stomach sank.

"No," he said, walking closer to his friend. He saw Groot's body slowly begin to dissolve into dust.

"No," Rocket said again, then faster, "No, no, no! Groot!"

He reached out for his friend, knowing there was nothing he could do, but not knowing what else *to* do.

And Rocket knew nothing would ever be the same again.